The Magic Phone

Gary Welch

Illustrated by Wesley Lowe

and Gary Welch

Registration: TXu 1-934-217, December 15th, 2014

10987654321

Hard cover# 9780996157605
Soft cover# 9780996157612
eBooks ISBN# 9780996157629

The story of the magic phone is based on a dream that my daughter, Abigail, had in 2012.

Preface –

The Magic Phone is a story of a young girl "Abigail" who lives in a quaint little town on the south shore of Long Island. She's given a phone with powers that you've never imagined from a device that so many of us use everyday. This story will take you on a journey that has many subjects that children find very exciting. The novel includes adventure, fantasy, historical events, humor, mystery, science fiction, and suspense. The Magic Phone will take Abigail and you through time, both in the past and the future. The Magic Phone gives you the power to teleport anywhere around the world, defy physics as we know it, allowing her to fly, move, lift, or throw objects that weigh thousands of pounds, manipulate the weather, heal the sick, and so much more. Take an amazing journey with Abigail, the adventures are endless with the magic phone.

Table of Contents:

Chapter One

Abigail's first walk Into Bellport

It was a beautiful spring day in May when Abigail decided to head out and take her dog Buttercup for a walk. She just finished her breakfast and asked her mom if it would be ok to take the dog out for a walk. Her mother said "that was fine", but to be safe and not to stay out too long. Abigail replied "all right", put the leash on Buttercup, and headed out the door, ready to go on a little adventure. Abigail decided to walk a little further than usual making it all the way into downtown Bellport, a quaint little town on the south shore of Long Island. As she walked along the downtown street, she noticed a nice restaurant with a long front porch, and a small convenient store to the right. On the other side of the street was a little café where folks would meet and have a cup of coffee and a bagel. As she continued down the street, Abigail noticed a woman wearing a beautiful red dress and red hat who was walking in the opposite direction towards her. Just then, Buttercup broke away and ran up to the woman, wagging her tail and standing up on her hind legs as if asking for attention. Abigail told Buttercup to get down, but she didn't, and continued to wag her tail and lick the woman. The woman told the little girl that it was OK, and that she liked dogs, and began petting Buttercup. Abby could tell that this woman really liked her dog; she began talking to the dog and asked Buttercup if she was having a nice day. Buttercup continued to wag her tail and lick her hand, while the woman pet her. Abigail apologized to the woman for Buttercup jumping up on her, and being so persistent on getting attention. The woman said, "that was all right". The woman then asked her what her name was and she replied "Abigail". She told her that Abigail was a beautiful name and asked her what her plans were for the day? Abigail replied that she was taking her dog for a walk and exploring Bellport for the first time by herself. The woman told her "that sounds like a lot of fun". She then stood up and told Abigail to be careful and have a great day. Abigail smiled and told the lady that she would, and to have a good day too. The woman continued on her way down the street, drawing some attention from the local folks.

As Abigail continued on her journey, she began to look around to see what else was on Main Street. A little further down on the right, she saw a store that sold mobile phones, which she hadn't noticed in the past and became intrigued by it. She had always wanted a phone, but her mother and father wouldn't let her have one. They would say "Abigail, you don't need a phone, because you have a phone at school and a phone at home, and if you are in the car with us, we have a phone that you can use". Abby rolled her eyes just thinking about this! But, she did understand her parent's point of view, even though her older brother and sister had one! Her brother Chad was thirteen and her sister, Shelby, was fourteen and somehow they had convinced mom and dad to buy them a phone. Abigail felt that she was old enough now, and was ready for a phone.

So, she decided to go into the store and buy one herself. Once inside the store, she met a nice man, who welcomed her to the store. He asked her what her name was and she replied Abigail. He said, "it's nice to meet you Abigail, and what is your dog's name"? She replied, "her name is Buttercup, and she's a Jack Russell". He bent down and scratched Buttercup on the back; you could tell that Buttercup was enjoying the attention, because her front legs came up off the ground and onto his leg to get closer. The man leaned over a bit further towards Buttercup, telling her what a good dog she was and Buttercup gave him several licks on his cheek. The man began to laugh and was enjoying this little dog. He then stood back up and asked how he could help her today.

Abigail began to ask a lot of questions about the phones; the kind of questions that you would expect a ten-year-old girl would ask. You know, can I call my mom or dad? Can I text my brother and sister? Can I get on the Internet and can I play games on it? Oh, and I like to listen to music on my brother's phone, can the phone do that too? The man took a liking to Abigail and Buttercup, who was being a good dog and listening to the two talk about these phones. The man asked Abby if she would take care of the phone? Abby said absolutely! The man then asked her if she would protect the phone so that nobody would steal it? Abigail told the man "yes, I will keep it in my pocket or my little purse that is the perfect size for the phone". The nice man then asked, "do you have enough money to buy a phone and hook it up to the network"? Abigail reached into her little purse and saw that she had ten dollars and seventy five cents.

She began to realize that she would not have enough money to buy the phone, something that she didn't even think about prior to entering the store. Her eyes grew sad as she looked slowly down at the ground and then her head began to drop, looking down at Buttercup. She didn't know what to say; she was embarrassed now. She looked back up at the man and said with a soft but quivering voice "I'm sorry mister, but I don't have enough money and I don't even know what a network is". Abigail apologized to the man for taking up so much of his time and said that she would leave. The man began to chuckle a little bit, further embarrassing Abigail. He replied, "I'm not laughing at you". "Don't be embarrassed; I think you're sweet and you're a good girl". "Listen, why don't you and Buttercup come in to the next room". "I want to show you something very special, that you may really like".

Abigail asked the man what his name was and he apologized for not introducing himself; he said that his name is Pete. I've lived here in Bellport all of my life, and this is my friend's store, I'm just helping him out this weekend, because he wanted to take a vacation for the week. How about you Abby, how long have you lived in Bellport? She replied, "I've lived here all my life too, except that I'm only ten years old", while Pete was in his seventies by now. Pete told her that there are a lot of phones out here in the showroom, but I have two really cool phones that aren't for sale, but I'll show them to you anyway. So, he brought her into a room that had some strange electronic devices in it that she had never seen before. She thought that it looked kind of like a laboratory.

Pete showed her some of the tools in the room. He showed her a spectrum analyzer that he used to tune the frequencies for the phones and a multi-meter that he used to check for the amperage, voltage, and resistance in circuits. Abigail thought this stuff was really cool, and was learning so much. Pete turned on the spectrum analyzer and tuned it to a few different frequencies, and on occasion, you could hear radio stations, strange atmospheric noises, and even cell phone conversations between two people. She told Pete that he was very smart, and how did he learn all of this stuff? He chuckled and told her that he would tell her that some other time. Pete told Abigail that he had a special phone for her that she wouldn't have to pay for, because someone had ordered the phone and never came in to pick it up. This person wanted her name engraved on the back, and guess what her name was? Abigail said she had no idea; Pete told her that the person's name was the same as hers. Her eyes opened as wide as they could and she said "no way, really?" Pete smiled and said yes and that this phone was meant for her! I want this to be my gift to you.

Pete walked over to a table with more lab equipment on it, along with two phones that were identical. Pete pointed to one of them and said to Abigail, this is a very special phone that I want to give you, but you must promise to keep it safe and use it with only good intentions. I will even take care of all the network charges for you so you won't have to pay a bill each month. He took the phone on the right and turned it over revealing the engraving "Abigail". He put it in a box, wrapped it up, and gave it to Abby.

Pete said, "Enjoy this very special gift from me and please be careful to protect it, and never lose it". "This phone can do things that only one other phone can do on earth. When you first start up the phone, it will walk you through a few instructions. Also, before you start using the phone, I want you to read the MDF instructions and become familiar with the phone and how it works. Abigail agreed, thanked Pete, and gave him a big hug. Off she went, heading straight home with Buttercup at her side. Pete picked up the other phone and walked down to the trophy and gift shop. He told the owner that he liked the way he engraved the other phone, and that he wanted to have "Pete & Tillie" engraved on his phone. When he saw the engraving, it pleased Pete and made him smile.

Abigail made her way through Bellport and down a few roads. As soon as she got home, she opened the present and pulled out the phone. It was a nice slim cell phone that looked really cool. She turned it over to look at her name again, and couldn't believe that this was her phone! The front and back looked very plain and except for the engraving the only other thing that she saw was a small square lens on the front and back. The shape of the phone was quite odd to her and she had never seen a phone look quite like this before. The phone seemed to fit the contours of her right hand.

On the left side of the phone there were two curves and a button on the top smaller curve, and on the right side of the phone there were four curves that were perfect for her fingers to slide onto. The front, sides, and back all shined like titanium, except for the right side of the phone where there were four inlays of what appeared to be glass. She put the phone into her right hand and it fit her hand almost perfectly; maybe, slightly big for her hand, but otherwise a perfect fit.

Abigail pushed the button on the side and the phone came alive. She saw the titanium front change into a liquid clear screen, and after about five seconds the screen disappeared revealing the titanium front again. Abigail powered up the phone again and the first thing that came up was a security screen. The screen instructed her to point the camera to her right eye. When she did this, the phone emitted a red beam of light that scanned her eye. After the first security check, the phone spoke for the first time and asked her to think of a word or phrase that she could use as another way to activate the phone.

Abigail thought about this for a few minutes and came up with the word "Buttercup", a name that she would never forget. The phone responded by saying that, if you want the phone to start up, you would need to scan your eye or state that word and only her voice would activate the phone. No other voice will activate this phone. The phone continued to lead her through the set up. The phone asked if she was at home, she replied 'yes'. The voice then told her that these coordinates are now designated as her home and that if she ever got lost, all she had to do was say home and the phone would get her back. Abigail thought that was a really cool feature. The phone asked if there were any phone numbers she would like to store in her address book. Abigail said yes and she typed in her mom and dad's numbers. The phone stated that the setup was complete and if she wanted to refer to the owner's manual, tap on the icon "MDF".

Once this was completed the main screen was displayed. Abigail noticed that it had a few special apps on it that were unusual; apps that she had never seen before on her older brother's and sister's phones. Two of these apps were called Magic Wand App and Planet Earth, along with the MDF icon. The rest of the phone seemed normal, like other phones she had seen in the past. She had an icon for texting, weather, maps, calendar, camera, contacts, oh and yes, a phone so she could call someone. After all, a phone should be able to call someone. She noticed that there wasn't a charger or earphones, but a device that attached to her ear with a microphone built in, and at the tip it was decorated with a pink stone that looked like an earring.

Abigail heard a noise coming down the hallway. It was her mother! Oh no Abby thought and put the phone into her nightstand. Her mom came into the room and asked her what she was doing. She said "nothing". So, her mom asked if she would like some lunch? Abigail said sure and they went into the kitchen together. She asked if she could have a hot pocket and her mom said sure. Her mom made a sandwich for herself and the hot pocket for Abigail.

They sat down at the table and got to talk for a while. Susan, Abigail's mom, then asked, what did you do this morning? She began to tell her mom about her walk into downtown Bellport, and all the stores that she saw; but, she left out the part about visiting with Pete at the phone store. She was sure that her mom would be mad if she got a phone and didn't ask for permission. Abigail told her mom that she would like to walk back into town with her, but she would like to walk all the way down to the great south bay. Her mother thought that was a great idea, and they agreed to visit downtown Bellport and the bay real soon.

After lunch, Abigail ran back into her bedroom and took the phone out. When she clicked the start button, it showed a photo of an eye. Abby had no idea what this was, and the phone turned off. So Abby pressed the start button again, and the eye came up on the screen. What's with the eye she exclaimed? Then, she realized that she had to put the phone up to her eye or say Buttercup. So she clicked on the start button again and put the lens up to her eye; then, a red light scanned her eye, and the phone turned on. Then, the phone asked if she would like an additional security test on start up that could activate the features on the phone. So, Abigail said "yes". The phone asked that she hold the phone in her right hand and then press continue. Abby did this and the phone scanned her fingers where she grasped the phone. She could see red light being emitted from the right edge of the phone where her fingers were.

The phone then stated that the security scan was complete and that upon start up she could use the eye scan, voice activation, or the fingerprint/DNA scan to open up the phones features. Abigail turned off the phone and wanted to test the security to see if this really worked. So she clicked the start button and said "Buttercup". The phone turned on. Very cool she thought! She then turned the phone off and held the phone on the curvy edges and clicked the start button; the phone scanned her fingerprints and the phone opened up the main screen. How cool is this Abby thought? This phone is so much better than my brother or sister's phone!!

4D Training
Translator
Magic Wand
Calendar
Planet Earth
Gateway
Currency
Clothing
Weather

Chapter Two

Magic Phone's Features

Now that the phone was on, Abby decided to find out how to use these cool Apps. She remembered Pete saying to read the MDF; so, she tapped the MDF app and up came the Magic Data Files. Magic data files! What's this all about she thought. Within the MDF were features and instructions on how to use the Magic Phone. Abby saw a list of words that she could not believe. Am I really seeing this, she thought? She saw words like Magic Wand App, How to Fly, The Shield, Medic App, and Time Machine. There were many other items within the MDF, which she would need to read; the list was very long.

Abby had so many thoughts running through her head by now. Is this really magic or just a phone that has a lot of games in it? She scrolled down to a word that matched one of the apps on her main screen "Planet Earth". She tapped on the title "1.0 – Planet Earth:" and it hyperlinked her to that section of instructions. *The MDF instruction manual is located in the last chapter of the book. Below is an excerpt from the MDF chapter. Afterwards, refer to the MDF as you like, or you can read the entire chapter to understand all of the features of the phone.*

Abigail began to read the instructions.

1.0 – Planet Earth:

This application allows the user to view the world from your home or to see towns, cities, countries, and places you would love to visit, but never could before. Within the app are several buttons and fields that you can use to interact with the app. There is a Search field, Where Am I button, Go To button, and a Home button.

The search field allows you to Type in an address, a business, a town or a city, and the application will search for your request.

The "Where Am I?" button will show where you are located on the map.

1.1 - The "Go To" button will take you to this location, teleporting you there in the blink of an eye. Don't worry, when this button is activated, it will take you to a safe location in the area that you chose. If you plan on taking someone on your trip with you "Be Careful" you have to hold onto that person or hold their hand tightly. If you leave with someone, be sure to bring that person back home with you! It is advised, for safety reasons, to travel alone!

1.2 - The "Go Home" button is exactly what you think it means. When you press this button, the phone will return you safely to your home, or you can tell the phone "Go Home".

OMG, Abigail thought. She turned the phone off while smiling, but thinking at the same time that this isn't real. She put the phone into her nightstand drawer and ran outside where she saw her dad. He was in the garage working on his Shelby Mustang. She asked her dad what town grammy and grampa lived in? He said that they live in a small town called Bethel. "Abby, why do you ask", he said? She said that she was just thinking of them and would like to visit them soon. He replied by saying "we will go up to Maine this summer and get to visit for a week". She said, "OK" and ran off, back into her room. She pulled the phone out of her drawer and pushed the start button and said Buttercup. The phone turned on and she went to the app Planet Earth.

Upon start up, it asked her to confirm that the current location is her home? Abigail tapped on the yes button. The app then zoomed into her current location, showing a very detailed picture of her house and all the neighbors' houses too. She opened the search field and typed in the town of Bethel, Maine. The map moved quickly northward and there it was! Her jaw dropped open and her hands began to tremble. Is this going to really work, she thought? Or is this just a game? Her finger hovered over the "Go To" button. As her finger trembled, she accidentally hit the button, and with a whoosh, she was gone.

Awhile later, Abby's dad came in to the house and called for her. He looked all over, but couldn't find her. He found Susan and told her that Abby wanted me to get her when I pulled out a spark plug to show her how it works. That girl loves learning about cars and how things work. He asked Susan, if she knew where Abby was and she said that I saw her in her room earlier. They both began to search for Abigail, but she was nowhere to be found around the house; so, they decided to search the neighborhood. "I think we should start at her friend's house down the street". So, off her parents went to go find Abigail.

Within an instant Abigail was in Bethel; she suddenly appeared behind an old wooden building. She was trembling and very scared. She began to cry and was missing her mom and dad already. She thought for a minute and stared at the phone, not sure what to do. All of a sudden, this woman with a little boy and girl came up to her and asked if she was ok? Abigail replied, but still crying and upset, "I'm ok". The woman asked her if she was lost and where her parents were? Abby said that they were downtown and she was just walking around. The woman asked why she was crying then?

Abby thought for a second, knowing good and well she couldn't tell this lady that she traveled instantly to Bethel from New York. So, she said that her dog died and she was still sad about this. The lady felt bad and kneeled down to Abby, giving her a hug and said to her "everything will be alright honey". Abby said "yeah, she is in heaven now". The woman then asked if she would like to walk downtown to find her parents. Abby replied no thank you, I want to find my grammy and grampa, and the woman replied "ok sweetie, have a great day" and walked off with her two kids.

Abby began to look around and one of the first things she noticed was that a lot of people were dressed in very old clothes, clothes that people would wear in the eighteen hundreds, and some men wearing military uniforms who were carrying rifles. She heard some of them walk into the building that she was standing next to. She was intrigued. She then looked up at the building and saw a window, but it was higher than her. So, she pulled up a wooden bucket that was nearby and climbed onto it. In the window she could see a lot of people walking around and talking with each other. She heard a few of the people talking about the civil war. She thought, Oh No! I'm sure that I didn't push any buttons to go back in time, but everyone was dressed in old clothes, civil war uniforms, old guns, and old style hats. This can't be happening Abby thought. Then, one of the men inside saw her at the window and began to walk over to her. Abby jumped off the bucket and ran, as fast as she could, down the road. In a bit of a panic and short of breath, she ended up at the corner of Broad Street and Main where she began to walk with her head down, but her eyes looking up to see what was going on around her. Her pace was fast like she was trying to get away from someone. As she walked, she noticed how everyone was dressed, bewildered beyond belief. Everyone was dressed like her. What is going on she thought? This is weird! She lifted her head and began to feel like she fit in. She thought to herself, this is the Bethel that I remembered when visiting my grammy and grampa last summer.

Now, where do my grandparents live? How do I find them? I can't remember where they live! I know that they live up on a hill. Hmm, what is the name of that road? As she walked along the street, she saw a banner that said "Bethel During The Civil War". She realized that she didn't go back in time. The town was just reenacting the Civil War.

Abby thought back and began to concentrate on the task at hand. She had an idea! With the phone glued to her right hand, Abby clicked the start button and it scanned her fingerprints and opened up to the main screen. She went back into the app Planet Earth, and it showed her that she was in Bethel. She could see where she was, right on Main Street in Bethel. She began to scroll around the area; it took a few minutes, but she found the road that her grandparents lived on. She scrolled around some more and finally saw her grammy's house. Abigail ran behind one of the stores where nobody could see her. She placed the cursor next her grandparent's house and tapped on the "Go To" button. Within in a flash, she was back at home. What? She was home? What happened?

Oh my gosh, she thought. I accidentally hit the Go Home button. I really am not good with this phone yet, she thought. She began to look around for her parents. She saw her brother, Chad, in his room; he was playing a dumb game on his computer. Chad loved playing computer games and was good at those first person war games along with racing games. Chad was also quite athletic. He ran cross country, swam, and wrestled for his school.

Abby could hear her parents calling for her in the distance. It sounded like her daddy was yelling and it sounded like he was upset. So, she ran into the back yard and climbed up onto the hammock. She began to tremble again, knowing good and well that she was in trouble. Chad heard them yelling for Abby; so, he came out and said that he just saw her. Where did you see her, Phillip asked? I think she's in the back yard. Everyone ran into the back yard and found her lying in the hammock. Her father ran to her, grabbed her, and pulled her in close to him; he was crying. She had no idea that being gone like this would cause such grief. Her dad asked her where she had been. Abby felt bad, but didn't want to get into trouble. She said, "I've been here, just sleeping on the hammock". She could hear her father saying in a soft low voice "Thank you God, thank you God".

Chapter Three

The Calendar App

For the next few days, Abby kept the phone locked away in her jewelry box that she had on her nightstand. She felt overwhelmed about the phone, the capabilities that this phone has, traveling from one place to another, at the speed of light, and also lying to her parents about what she's been doing! She felt really bad about how she made her parents feel when they were out looking for her, and realizing that they were hurting inside, because they thought I was lost or abducted by a stranger.

Abigail didn't want to put her parents through this pain again and needed to find away not to let this happen again. But, at the same time, to be able to use the phone and it's magic. Abigail looked forward to going back to school on Monday. She needed to get back to doing some normal things again, to see her friends and teachers, and not think about what had happened over the last few days. Abby, loved school. Her teachers had made comments, on her report card and to her parents, that she was attentive in class, respectful of her teachers, and fellow students; that she was a leader, played fair, and always worked hard for the grades that she got. Abby's favorite subjects were math, english and history, and loved talking about these subjects to anyone who would listen.

On Monday, Abby headed back to school; she gave her mom and dad a kiss and a big hug and jumped on the bus. She couldn't wait for her friend Vanessa to get on the bus so she could talk with her and find out how her weekend was and just spend time with her. When Vanessa got on the bus, she sat down next to her friend Abby, and the two of them just smiled and never stopped talking about their weekends, but of course Abby left out the crazy stuff that happened. She did talk about taking her dog for a walk into Bellport and window-shopping, and hanging out with her family. She found out that Vanessa went into the city to see a play and stayed overnight in this grand Hotel. Abby thought that was amazing and would like to do that someday too.

When they both got to school, they said "until later", and went to their classrooms. Abigail's teacher did role call and began class; she then asked for the homework that they were supposed to do over the weekend. Abigail took hers out and handed it in. She was so glad that she did her homework Friday night before the weekend, because she would have never finished it if she had waited. She remembered her mom and dad telling her "Get your homework done first thing after school, and then you can go out and play".

The morning went real fast and the next thing Abigail knew was that it was time for lunch. She would always meet up with Vanessa for lunch and afterwards go out to the playground and swing as high as they could or go down the slide as many times as possible before the bell rang. Later that day, she was learning about the History of America. The teacher talked about the trials and tribulations of early America. She described how the pilgrims traveled so far across the Atlantic Ocean and had to work so hard just to stay alive. The teacher described all the taxes that the people had to pay to the British, and how they began to rebel against this taxation. Abby thought the tea party was a cool event and began to imagine this actually happening. She imagined taking over a ship in the middle of the night, taking its cargo of tea and throwing it overboard. Surely, this would anger the British, she thought.

Nevertheless, the teacher went on to describe the Revolutionary war, what the American's had against the British, and how they persevered against the British rule. The teacher told all the students that they would need to write a book report on an event that happened during the Revolutionary War. Abby began to think about what she wanted to write about and after careful deliberation, she decided that she would write about how the Continental Congress would deliberate whether to declare independence or concede to the British. When she got home, after school, she talked to her mom about the project and asked if she could help her out a little. Her mother told her that she would love to, because she loved American history.

She also began to tell Abigail a story about their family tree. She asked Abby if she knew that she was related to any famous people back during this time period? Abby replied "No". So her mom began to go back through the generations, starting with her father on up to the second president of the United States, John Adams. Abby's eye's widened and she said, "I'm related to John Adams"? How am I related to him, she asked. Her mother replied back, stating, "Yeah, he's your seventh great grandpa, and he had a lot to do with the Declaration of Independence. I think this project will be great for us to do together! Her mother asked Abby another question, “do you know who we named you after?” Well, Abby said, “no I don’t”. Her mother said that she was named after John’s wife, Abigail Adams. Her mother went on to say how smart Abigail Adams was and that she had a lot of influence on the direction her husband went in throughout his career in the Continental Congress and his presidency. Abby smiled and told her mom that she was proud to have a great name like Abigail.

Abby was also told that Mrs. Adams would write to John all of the time and advise him. When John was working on the Declaration of Independence, she wrote to him and told him not to forget about the women. She also told him that if we are to truly be free, we cannot have slavery in this country. This was way back in the seventeen hundreds when she said that, a true visionary for this country! Abigail was very happy that she asked her mom to help on this project and learned so much about her past and about John and Abigail Adams.

Later in the week, Abby began her book report. She started by researching all that she could about the Continental Congress; who was part of the congress and what states they were from. She found out that John Adams from Massachusetts was completely in support of Independence from the British and that he had to persuade many others from the congress, because of the fear they had that the British would kill everyone for revolting. After many months of negotiations, he was able to persuade the congress to declare independence, and on July 4th 1776, the Declaration of Independence was adopted. Abigail loved reading about the early years of our nation and her seventh great grandpa. She also loved reading about the letters John and his wife would write back and forth to each other. She noted how intelligent and articulate Abigail was with her writing, and agreed with her mother on what a great vision she had for her time.

After all of her reading, Abby had a better understanding of what the Fourth of July really meant. While thinking about this, she fell asleep on her bed. Her mom and dad came into her room and smiled at how Abigail was sleeping; she was lying back in the bed with books all around her. They cleaned up the small mess and tucked her into bed. That night, she began to dream about all that took place during the times of the Continental Congress and the Revolutionary war.

Abby found herself in a deep sleep and began to dream of living back in the days where the nations birth was about to occur. She found herself on a cobblestone street. She knew that something big was about to happen as she approached Carpenter's Hall, because she could hear all of the men inside arguing with loud voices. Something of great importance was being discussed! So, she made her way into the building and followed the sounds of the men. She approached a large door and listened in. She heard the men talking and then she heard the men agreeing on a plan. Each representative was asked to come up to sign the Declaration of Independence.

Peeking through the keyhole, she could see John Adams, his cousin Samuel, Thomas Jefferson, William Floyd, and many other men. This was it! The birth of America, she thought. The next thing that she knew was that the door opened up and knocked her backwards onto her bottom and then onto her back. Her eyes were closed and it appeared that she was knocked out cold. People began to gather around the young girl.

Abby was awakened from this deep sleep by her mom. The sun was up and it was morning already. Abigail was disoriented; she looked around as if she were lost, and realized that she was at home. She told her mom that she had this dream that felt so realistic, a dream where she went back in time and watched the continental congress signing the Declaration of Independence. She then got up and made her bed, got dressed for school, brushed her hair and ran out to have breakfast with her family. She got a bowl out of the cabinet and poured some cereal and milk into it. As she ate her breakfast with her mom, dad, and brother, she talked about all that she learned the night before, and how she couldn't wait to learn more about the signing of the declaration.

After breakfast, she put the bowl into the sink and ran into the bathroom to brush her teeth. When she was done, she grabbed her book bag and lunch and ran to the bus stop. She looked forward to seeing her friend Vanessa and sitting next to her on the bus. Abby wasn't very talkative today, she was thinking about living in the days of the revolutionary war again. She couldn't wait until history class, because she wanted to learn as much as she could about it.

The morning started off really slow and Abby couldn't wait to talk to her history teacher after lunch. When the bell rang, she hurried to the lunchroom and found her best friend Vanessa. They ate lunch together and after, went up to the dessert bar and bought an ice cream. They sat back down at the table to eat their ice cream and they began to talk about their summer, which was coming up real soon, and they only had a few more weeks left in school. Abigail talked about how she loved going to camp, because she would do archery, arts and crafts, swim, and go to lunch with her dad, who was only two blocks away from where she had camp. Vanessa said that she loved going on vacation, and this year, they were going to Florida. She looked forward to the amusement parks, going to the beach, and the barbecues in the back yard.

After their ice creams, they went out to the playground and played on the swings for a while. Then, the school bell rang; it was time to go to history. Abby ran to her locker and pulled out the history book and ran into the classroom. When the class started, her history teacher, Mr. Brenner, asked the class if they had any questions from the previous lesson. Abigail's hand flew up and she said that she had a question. Mr. Brenner asked her what her question was and she asked, "Why would a King want to rule a people from a country he didn't even live in"? He thought for a minute and pondered that question: "Maybe the King was upset that a lot of the people were leaving his land and moving to America, and he was going to control them no matter where they lived". Abby said that the settlers were trying to get away from the tyranny that was going on in Europe and now the government is following them to another land. She didn't think that was fair.

Her teacher agreed with her and said that life was very hard during those days, but American's persevered through the worst of times. Abby told Mr. Brenner that she would have fought for her freedom if she had to. As the class went on, Abby learned more about the revolutionary war and took as many notes as possible. She wanted to do well on her report so that she'd get an A, and learn more about her great grandfather at the same time.

At the end of the school day, when Abby got home, she headed straight for her bedroom and closed the door. She wanted to find out what other amazing things this phone could do. She took the phone out from her jewelry box and touched the start button, it scanned her fingerprints on her right hand and the main screen came up. She looked for an app that had anything to do with time travel, but couldn't find anything. She tapped on the Icon called Magic App and browsed through the many functions within it. She saw speed dial, shield, and flight school. She looked through other apps and saw: Gateway, Weather, Translator, Medic, Food & Water, Clothes, and Currency. She wanted to tap one of the icons, but held back from doing so, because she didn't know how to use these apps safely. She didn't want to use this phone improperly and get herself or someone hurt.

She remembered hearing her mom say one time to her dad, when he was building a bike for her, that he should have read the instructions first. Something happened while he was putting the bike together, where one thing was put on out of sequence. So, he had to take the bike a part and do it right, the second time. She remembered that the MDF app had a lot of instructions in it; so, she closed the magic app and opened up the MDF. She started looking around for time travel, because she wanted to travel back in time and see for herself, what it was like to live in the United States at the time it was born.

She looked up and down, but couldn't see anything that resembled time travel. However, she did scroll past the Calendar app a few times. She thought for a second or two and wondered if this was the app that could allow her to travel through time. She tapped on the words 2.0 - Calendar App and she was hyperlinked to the MDF instructions. *Please refer to the MDF chapter, 2.0.*

Abby could not believe that this phone could do so much; she was so excited to use it, but thought it would be best to have a chat with Mr. Pete. She went to the directory, in her phone, and found three entries, her mom, dad, and Pete & Tillie. Abby figured that Tillie must be Pete's wife, but wasn't sure. She tapped on Pete's name and the phone began to ring his number. After four rings, a woman with a soft voice came on and she said "hello Abigail". Abby said Hi and then asked if this was Tillie. The woman replied "Yes, I'm Tillie; how do you like the phone so far"? Abby smiled and said "I love it and can't wait to learn more about it". Tillie asked her to be careful with the phone, and not to let anyone know about it, unless you could completely trust them with your secret. She also said, that if anyone approaches you and asks about the phone, don't tell them anything! Tillie went on about the phone and how it took Pete so many years to create this phone and that it was the accumulation of all he learned in each field of science over the last 50 years.

Tillie asked Abby if she knew anything about Pete? Abby said that he works at the phone store and lived in Bellport all of his life. Other than that, she didn't know anything else; but, tell me all about him, she exclaimed. Tillie laughed a bit and said, I'll tell you a little bit about Pete, but there is just too much to tell if you want to know everything.

She said that Pete was a very smart man, a genius in fact. He was a scientist, physicist, and an electrical engineer who had worked at Brookhaven National Laboratory for many years. He was an inventor of many amazing devices over his career, but the phone was a culmination of what he had learned and experimented with throughout his entire adult life. "Abby, you must be a very special person, for

Pete to give you one of his phones". How did you talk him into giving you the phone? Abby told Tillie that she wasn't sure, "we just talked for awhile, and I think he liked my dog too". Tillie laughed and said that I know you want to talk to Pete and I'll put him on for you. "It was nice to talk with you"! Abby said the same and that she would like to meet her real soon. Tillie said that would be great and looked forward to it.

Tillie then handed the phone over to Pete and he said "hello". Abby said "hi" and asked him how he was. Pete replied, "Oh, I'm doing just fine" but I've been worried about you Abby and was hoping that you were all right. Abby said that she's been fine and learning more and more about the phone and was amazed at all it could do. She asked Pete, how did you do this, how did you create such an amazing device? He chuckled a bit and told her, I'm not sure. I seemed to have invented a lot of individual things over a long period of time and then I put all of the technologies together into this small amazing phone.

He asked her if she found the charger yet? And she said, "no, there wasn't one in the box". That's right Pete replied, there's no charger; within the phone is a small amount of uranium that creates a temperature gradient and turns a very small generator; this will power the batteries that I created a few years ago. The power supply should last for at least 100 years. Pete told Abby not to worry, the phone is very safe and sealed so well that no one would be able to detect any radiation from this phone.

Pete asked Abby what questions she had about the phone? Abby didn't know where to start; she had so many questions to ask Pete. Then, Abby heard something at her door; she looked but didn't see anything, except that the door was cracked open. She got up and closed the door. She continued with Pete and asked if she could meet with him this Saturday? Pete said that would be fine, but it wouldn't be a good idea to meet at the store. He told Abby, when we get off the phone, go to my contact information. There, you will see my address. Tap on my address and the app, Planet Earth, will come up and locate my house. The phone will give you step-by-step instructions or you can just teleport here! That's more fun than walking as he chuckled. Just give me a call before you come, so that Tillie and I are ready.

Abby put her phone away into her jewelry box, and ran into the bathroom to brush her teeth and get ready for bed. When she was done, her mom and dad came into her bedroom and they all said a prayer together. While Abby was praying, she asked God to take care of her family, grammy and grampa, her church family, and to watch over Pete and Tillie and to keep them safe. Abby's mom and dad looked up at each other bewildered. As they were leaving Abby's room, they began to ask why she would be praying for Pete and Tillie? They both said that they haven't seen them in about six months, and how has Abby been in touch with them. Susan said that she would look into it tomorrow.

Chapter Four

The Family's Beginning to Notice Things

Later in the night, Abby's brother, Chad, came out of his bedroom and snuck into Abby's bedroom. He had been looking into her room earlier, through the crack of the door, and listened in on the conversation that she had with Pete on the phone. He wanted to find out more about this phone. He had seen her put it away in the box on top of her nightstand, earlier that night; so, he opened up the box and saw the phone. He took it into his room and began to investigate what this phone was all about. He pressed the on button and an eye came up. He wasn't sure what this was, but he had heard Abby say Buttercup a few days back. So, he said "Buttercup". The phone replied "Access Denied". The phone then shut off.

He pushed the on button again and he saw the eye come up, but still wasn't sure what to do with the phone. It would not come on! As he continued to try to get into this phone, he put it in his right hand and worked his fingers into the grooves activating the fingerprint scanning. When he pushed the start button, the red light began to emit from the sides of the phone. He dropped the phone onto the floor and his heart began to race. Chad began to sweat a little and by now, he was kind of afraid of this phone. It was too different from any other phone he had seen before. Chad got up the nerve to try it again and put it into his right hand. He pushed the start button, and the phone scanned his fingerprints. The phone said "Access Denied". Chad was starting to loose it. He couldn't get into the phone! He tried one more time holding the phone a little differently than before and when he hit the start button, the eye came up again. "Oh my gosh", Chad said. What is this? He thought a little bit and decided that this might be a pupil scan.

He had heard about this type of security in a class he took in school. He pushed the button and placed the phone's lens up to his eye. A red light scanned across his eye and just after that a very bright burst of light shot out of the phone, directly into his eye. Chad let out a shriek from the pain this caused him, and immediately fell asleep. The phone still in his hand when it said "Access Denied". Just then, Pete was in the room. The phone had alerted him of a security violation; so, he teleported to the phone's position. He took the phone from Chad and quickly placed it back into Abigail's jewelry box. Then, within a flash, Pete was gone.

After school the next day, Abby was outside playing in the back yard when Chad came into the house, he snuck into Abby's bedroom again. He slowly opened up the jewelry box and looked in. The phone was not there! Chad was becoming frustrated and didn't know what to do. So, he went outside and confronted his little sister. "Abby, what did you do with that phone of yours"? "I want to know where you got it and what's a Magic Phone? She said that it was none of his business about her phone and to leave her alone. He kept on and on about it. The only thing she would tell him was that her friend Pete gave her the phone.

Chad walked back into the house at the same time that his dad and stepsister came in. He said "Hi" to the both of them and then grabbed Shelby by the hand and ran into his room with her. Shelby and Chad are about the same age, where Shelby lives with her mom about half of the time. Shelby likes to ride horses, and she likes to read and draw a lot of Anime characters, although, she doesn't have a lot of time for that, because she usually has so much homework to do. Chad began to tell Shelby all about the phone and the crazy things he heard it could do. He even mentioned that it scanned his eye and blasted him with a burst of light, blinding him for a while. He asked her if she knew anything about it, or if she had ever heard of a phone that had so much security? She said that she hadn't heard Abby say anything about it. But, she told Chad that she would look into it though.

After dinner, Shelby and Abby went into their bedroom together. Shelby told Abby that Chad had mentioned her new phone. Abby just rolled her eyes and said "yes, I have a phone and it was given to me by my friend Pete". Shelby asked who Pete was and why he would give her such a cool phone for free, and who was paying the monthly fees? After all, mom and dad said they weren't going to buy you a phone until you were in high school. Abby began to tell her about how she met Pete at the phone store in downtown Bellport, and that "I think that he felt bad that I didn't have enough money to buy a phone". Plus, he said that a woman ordered the phone and had her name engraved on the back, but never picked it up, and guess what her name was? Shelby said "Abigial". "Yes, she replied and she said that Pete told her that this phone was meant for me. Abby told her that Pete loved Buttercup too.

Shelby asked how he knew Buttercup? Well, when I walked into Bellport that day, I brought Buttercup, and Buttercup came into the store with me. Buttercup was sniffing around the store and began to sniff Pete when he walked up to me. Buttercup's front two paws went up onto his pant's leg and she was begging for him to scratch her back. Buttercup took a liking to Pete, right from the beginning. Pete thought that Buttercup and I were great together, and he just liked us! Then, he said that he had a very special phone that he would like to give me, but I had to keep it safe and not let anyone know about it, unless I could really trust them; he said that he would even pay the monthly fees for me. Shelby said that was really nice of him, to do all of that for her.

Shelby asked Abby, if she had her number in the phone? Abby said no, but pulled out the phone and began to put in the number. Shelby didn't see Abby scan her eye, get her fingerprints scanned, or even say Buttercup. It was still pretty bright out and Shelby couldn't tell whether the phone scanned her fingerprints or not. She thought that it could be more visible at night. Anyway, Abby asked Shelby for her number and put it into her contacts list. She asked Shelby what her mom's address was too. She put in all of the information and began to write her first text to her sister. It read "Hey sis, how r u"? Shelby replied "Good, what's up with u"? They both played around, texting each other, and even video chatting for the first time together.

Shelby never really asked Abby anymore about the phone, and Abby felt, inside, that if she could confide in someone, it would be her big sister. Later, Chad came up to Shelby and asked if she found out anything about Abigail's phone? Shelby said that it was just a regular Smartphone and nothing else. Chad rolled his eyes, even more frustrated, and went into his bedroom. He knew that there was more to this phone than that, and wanted to find out what it was.

Time flew by that week and it was Saturday. Her dad was out in the garage tinkering on his car and her mom was in the back yard cleaning up the garden. Abby went outside and asked her dad if it was ok to go over to her friend's house. He said sure, but to be back in a few hours. She said, "thank you dad", and ran up to give him a big hug. She said, "You're the best dad in the whole world"! She went into her room and pulled the phone out of her pocket. She pulled up Pete's info and gave him a call. After he answered the phone, she asked "Are you ready for me to come over"? He said "sure"! "When do you think you'll be here"? He heard nothing! He asked a few times and then he heard, I'm here already! He turned around and there she was. While on the phone, she had opened the contacts list, tapped on Pete's address, up came Planet Earth, and she tapped Go To! And Wha lah, here I am, faster than a SR71 spy plane in a nose dive! Pete laughed out loud and shook his head back and fourth. He told Abigail that she was learning how to use his phone really fast and was quite impressed with her progress. Abby smiled, and said lets get started!

Pete told Abby, "follow me, you sneaky little girl" He took her into the family room and wanted to introduce her to his wife Tillie. As they walked in, Tillie looked around her chair and asked, "Well who is this"? "This must be Abigail"! They all talked for a while and Pete and Tillie told Abby all about Bellport for the past sixty years or so.

Pete, Tillie, and Abby then went down to his laboratory. He told Tillie that he was going to show her how to use that silly old phone, with a smile on his face.

Chapter Five

Close Encounter

As Abby walked down into the basement, she began to notice a lot of equipment. You know the equipment that I'm talking about, the equipment that you would see in a mad scientist's laboratory! He showed Abby diagrams of several components within the phone and tried to describe how things worked. He talked to her in a proud tone of voice, and was excited to talk to someone about his invention. Pete told Abby "I can trust you, I can feel it". So, don't tell anyone else about the stuff I discuss with you, unless you're absolutely sure you can trust them, like I trust you! She agreed with Pete and he began to talk more about the phone. He told her that this phone was on a network tied into the natural forces within the universe, and that she could talk to anyone on this planet and on another planet as a matter of fact. He told her that as she learned more about the phone, that new apps would become available.

Pete began to tell her how the phone stayed charged all the time, and Abby said "I know, you told me already". It's powered by a small atomic charge. Pete laughed and said "oh, I forgot I told you already, you are too darn smart for your age little girl". She said that this phone could do incredible things that go beyond invention. So, how did you really figure this all out? He paused for a while and began to explain. First, you need to know that information comes to you in small packets, and you need to write it down, and document these packets of information. As you accumulate your writings, you will be able to see things that you never imagined. Second, he told her that about forty years ago, he was working on many experiments that included many facets into physics, electrical engineering, and computing. He said that he was able to figure out many new ways of harnessing energy, creating smaller and smaller circuitry, and even communicating over wireless networks. Pete began to talk about messages that he had sent out over the past forty years or so on millions of frequencies, throughout the universe. He figured that if he could contact a people with a higher intelligence, he would learn a lot more than he would with many of his co-scientists. He thought that it was a far shot, but kept on sending these messages out into space, twenty-four hours a day, seven days a week.

While this was going on, he kept experimenting on hundreds of projects, and at some point in time, he forgot all about the messages being sent out into space. He continued with his work and made great strides for the government and the department of energy. He said that it took about twenty years. What took twenty years Abby exclaimed? Well, I was visited. Visited by who? Abby shouted! Pete said that his message was answered! Someone answered your messages, Abby asked? Pete replied "yes". Abby became very excited and asked Pete to tell her all about who answered the message and who visited you.

Pete agreed and started to tell Abby about his close encounter with aliens from space. Abby was focused on everything Pete had to say. Pete continued with his story, telling Abby that one very quiet night, a spacecraft had flown into the earth's atmosphere, and landed at the laboratory. Internal alerts were sounded and security rushed to the sight of the landing spacecraft. Pete could hear all of the commotion on the radios and took off to see what was going on. When he saw the spacecraft, he realized that this might be a result of what he had done, and that this spacecraft had followed his signals that he had been sending out into space. "Oh my", he thought. "I'm in big trouble"!

The spacecraft had settled on the ground and sat silent for about twenty minutes. From what appeared to be a solid metallic wall of the ship, two parallel seams appeared horizontally first and then vertically, which formed the shape of a rectangle. This was a door that opened and then descended to the ground. Abby asked Pete "were you scared"? Pete laughed and said, "shoot yes I was scared". "Would you be scared"? Abby said, "shoot yes" and smiled. Pete continued with his story and talked about how a person came out of the craft. The person stood about 5 feet tall and looked quite normal, except his skin was very white, like he hadn't seen the sun in years. He had hair too, not quite as much as we have, but it was straight and pure white.

The alien took out a device from a pocket in his space suit and began to push on it with his two thumbs. Within a few seconds another alien came out. They both began to walk towards the people who had started gathering around the ship. As they both approached, Pete said that he noticed that their eyes were slightly bigger than ours, but not by much. The person leading out of the space ship took out his device again and began to push a few buttons and held it out. As he approached the small crowd of scientists, the guards drew their weapons. The two aliens stopped and waited still, with the exception that they were tapping away at this device with their thumbs. It appeared that a thin film of energy appeared around them, like a forcefield. They both looked up at the crowd and in English stated, we would like to speak with the earthling named Pete, and learn more about your world.

Pete said that he hesitantly looked around and wasn't sure what to do, but then took a step forward and replied, "I am Pete". The two aliens turned to Pete and one of them said "thank you Pete for your messages". We have been listening to them for a long time and we are grateful that we made it to your planet. Pete told the two people "Welcome to planet Earth". The two aliens said that they would like to discuss some of your calculations and theories regarding extended space travel, nano-materials, and sustainable energy sources. Pete told everyone to stand back and took the aliens into his laboratory and remained in this area for months. When he descended down into his bunker, security began the task of covering up the spaceship with camouflage, and later moving it to an undisclosed location at Brookhaven Lab.

Abby was beside herself and couldn't believe all that Pete was saying. "I can't believe that there are people who live in outer space"! She asked Pete, "what did you do with the people who came out of the space ship"? Why were you in the lab for months? Pete told Abby that he learned so much from those two people while he was with them. They taught me so much about physics and how to defy the physics in our universe, and I was actually able to teach them a few things or two. But, not as much as what they taught me, that's for sure. In fact, the device that the alien had in his hand was actually a device very similar to your phone, except it was primarily used for communicating, at the time. They used that device to talk to each other and to their base on a planet far away. When they were exiting the aircraft, the two aliens would use their thumbs to type in sentences, which would allow them to communicate with each other, without talking. That's what we call texting these days.

Abby asked, "when did this happen anyway"? Pete told her that this took place in the late 60's. Abby could not believe all this. This is crazy Pete!!! Yeah, I know dear, it is hard to believe, but it did happen. Abby asked, how long were you able to hang out with the alien guys? Pete replied that he spent about three months with them, and by the way, one of them was male and the other was a female. "Oh yeah?" Abby said, and did they fly back into space and go home? Pete held silent for a little while, and a tear began to develop under his eye. He said, "no Abby they didn't get to go back home. They actually became sick and our medical team, here at the lab, tried to get them better.

The two of them died from bacteria that their bodies weren't used to. They were able to contact their planet and report back that we were to be considered friends. They sent back a lot of information that they had learned here on earth. They also reported that they were getting sick and weak and that the medical team was doing all they could to help them. The first to die was the female, and when this happened the man sent a message, to Gmack, indicating that one astronaut was deceased and he would not make it much longer.

Pete said that the second astronaut from Gmack had died within a week of the first dying. We were able to learn a lot about their anatomy and physiology, and how they lived, through the autopsy that was performed on them, and a few months of medical research. But, the Department of Defense found out about the visit and took the spacecraft and the bodies from us. Pete told Abby that we need to stop talking about this; we only have so much time today to learn some features of this phone. Abby asked one more question "what and where is Gmack"? Pete answered, "Gmack is a planet that circles a sun just like our earth and it's about one thousand light years away from our solar system". Wow, Abby thought, that's a long ways away! She thought how could those two astronauts travel such far distances? That is something I will have to ask Pete later, she thought.

Pete pulled out his phone to begin showing Abby how to use the calendar feature. He told Abby that we are about to go on an adventure. He said that I've been doing this for about five years now and I've become pretty good at traveling through time, both back in time and into the future. Pete asked Abby to take her phone out and follow along with him. He opened up his phone via the pass phrase of "Upton". Abby smiled and pushed on her start button and said "Buttercup". Both phones were on. Abby glanced over at Pete's phone and her jaw dropped. She asked Pete how he had so many Apps on his phone and she only had a few. He told her that there are many Apps that can go with this phone. Yours are quite advanced for anyone; but, you have a lot of possible upgrades in the future, if you remain disciplined with how to use the phone properly, and that you can respect the power of this phone. He told her that as she learns the features of the phone, he would send upgrades based on her level of experience.

Pete stopped his tutoring session for a few minutes to tell her something. "Listen" Pete said! I am able to monitor what you are doing with this phone and it's not to listen in or watch your personal conversations with your family or friends, it's to protect you and watch how you use the device. For instance, if I see that you are back in time and you're having trouble, I can help you get back home! Another reason why I need to monitor the phone, is incase someone takes it from you. If this were to happen, I will need to locate the phone and either move through time or use the speed dial app to get it back. Abby asked what "speed dial was"? He told her that he would get to that a little later. Oh, and one other reason for monitoring is that when I see that you're ready for the upgrades, I will send them to you.

Abby hugged Pete and thanked him for being such a wonderful man and friend. Pete smiled and said, "alright, let's get started on some time travel. OK, open up the magic App and tap the icon clothing. Once you have done this, put in the time period that you will be traveling to. For training purposes, I want you to put in 1969. Abby typed in 1969 and a menu of clothing came up for that time period. They both picked out their clothes for this year and Pete instructed Abby to click save, and Abby saved her selection. Pete told Abby that if she doesn't pre-select clothing the App will put her in clothing from that time period and she may not like what it picks! Abby asked Pete "how does the App know what size I am? Ah, the next step is to enter your age, and the clothing will be appropriate for your age. If the clothing is too small, then increase the age by a year and the clothing will be slightly bigger. Pete told Abby that she could tweak the size by adjusting the age up or down. Abby put in eleven years old since she was a little bigger than most ten-year-old girls.

Now, Pete asked her to close out of this App and go to the calendar. Down at the bottom of the screen, there is only one active tab that you can press, it's the set date tab. Press this tab and I want you to scroll back to 1969 and enter your father's birth date. She entered in his birth date. Now, put in the time of 11 AM. She did this and tapped on the done tab. Pete stated that the next screen is for her safety and she would either leave the default "return back home time" or enter another time. Pete said that the default time is forty-eight hours, but I want you to enter two hours. Abigail entered two hours into the return home menu.

All right, Pete said, "you are doing great". Now, once you have entered the automatic return home time, the next window is "Location". Tap on that icon. See how the calendar app disappears into the middle of the phone and the Planet Earth appears from the same place? I want you to pick a location. Type in this address and Abby did as Pete instructed her to; now, put in San Diego California. Abby followed the instructions. Pete asked Abby to tap enter and she saw the App quickly move to this location. Once it was locked in on the address in San Diego, a blue cross that pulsed appeared.

Now, Abby, tap the done button. When she tapped this button, Planet Earth disappeared as if it was being sucked into the middle of the phone and the calendar emerged as if being pulled back up from the depths of the phone. How cool is this Abby thought! Now Abby, do you see how the "Go To" button is active. Abby replied "yes, I can see that". Pete told her that when she taps that button, she will be transported to the address and that time period, and the clothes she had selected will be on her when she gets there. Oh, and if you take someone with you during your time travel, make sure they are holding onto you tightly, and don't worry, the App will pick out some clothes for them too.

Pete had said "So, while you were entering all this information, I had entered the same info on my phone. What I want you to do Abby is watch me tap the Go To tab and I will vanish. When that happens, then it's your turn. I will meet you there"! Pete gave Abby a little kiss on the cheek and then tapped the Go To tab, and Whoosh, he was gone. Oh my gosh, Abby thought. Oh no, now I have to tap the tab! Abby closed her eyes and tapped on the one active tab, and with a whoosh, she was gone too.

Abby felt the whoosh and thought the feeling was similar to the waves pushing her around that she had experienced when on vacation at Myrtle Beach. Then, she felt a sense of acceleration like she was in a jet airplane or a rocket ship. She found herself in this spiral tunnel traveling so fast. She could see through the tunnel and out into the universe, millions of stars all around her, and then all of a sudden a feeling of deceleration and then bright light where she found herself, in what must be, San Diego.

She was now standing, somehow maintaining her balance; she looked up and saw a gold and white Blue Moon trailer. It had an awning on the side and some toys and a motorcycle underneath it. She turned around and there was Pete, smiling at her. "You made it"! Abby smiled and said "yes, yes I did". So Abby, I want you to look in the back yard; do you see that lady and man back there? They are your father's mom and dad, your two grandparents! That is Mary and Gary. Abby felt a rush of warmth over her body and was so excited to see her grandparents for the first time. Pete said that they are setting up a table for your father's sixth birthday party. Pete and Abby walked across the street and watched the activities from a far. They began to see people walking and driving up to the trailer and going into the yard.

A few minutes later, a girl about seven years old came out of the front door to the trailer. She brought out a pitcher of what appeared to be Kool-aid. Then she saw him! A boy came out of the front door of the trailer. A six-year-old boy, who jumped out of the doorway avoiding all of the steps, landing on the cement porch and taking off towards the back where so many others were. That was her dad. OMG, Is that my dad Pete? He smiled and said yes, that is your dad. "He's so cute she said" They both began to laugh and enjoy the time of watching her father have his sixth birthday party.

Abigail was able to watch him play pin the tale on the donkey, hit the pinyatta with a bat, and play bobbing for apples. She later heard all the parents and kids singing happy birthday. She ran back across the street by the front of the yard, and watched as her father blow out the candles. After blowing out the candles, her father smiled and began to laugh. As he looked around, he saw this ten-year-old girl standing at the edge of his yard. They looked right at each other and then his mom started to cut the cake, distracting him long enough so that Abigail and Pete could walk away from everyone's sight. Pete took her by the hand and told her to hang on as he tapped the "Return Home" tab. She did as Pete asked and they disappeared at the same time.

They both arrived at Pete's house. Abby was crying and told Pete that she didn't want to go. She wanted to see her dad along with her grandma and grandpa longer. He brought her in close to him and told her that she can't stay there, that's not your time honey. But, wasn't it nice to get to see them? Yes, it was, and Pete "thank you so much for allowing me to experience this"! You have given me such a great gift, and I don't know why I deserve all of this from you? Pete told her that she was welcome and that her positive and respectful attitude, is what drew him in, to be giving. You are a sweet person, who cares about others, and I liked that. That is why I wanted to give you this gift. Pete then told Abby, that it was two in the afternoon and that she had better get home before her parents started to look for her.

Abby agreed, gave Pete a big hug, took her phone out, and went to planet earth, and tapped return home. With a whoosh, she was back home in her bedroom. Abby put her phone into her jewelry box and turned to the door. That's when she saw her sister, Shelby, sitting up in bed, with a book in her lap, and her mouth wide open. Abby froze and didn't know what to say. All Shelby could say was "What in the heck just happened?" Abby didn't say anything, not knowing what she could do to get out of this, she just stared back at Shelby. Shelby asked again "Abby, what is going on"? "You just appeared out of thin air"! Chad told me some weird stuff was happening, so what is going on? Abby told her that she wasn't supposed to tell. Pete told me not to say anything to anyone. Shelby said "Not even your sister?" Abby told Shelby that she could only tell someone whom she could trust completely. A person who would promise not to tell anyone about the magic that it can do, no matter what! Shelby asked who is Pete anyway? Abby replied by saying Pete is the man who gave me the magic phone. "What is the magic phone?" Tell me about it, Shelby replied.

Abby told Shelby that she would have to promise not to tell anyone, not even the police! Shelby agreed and told her sister that she loves her very much and would protect her secret. Abby began to tell her the story about the phone and a lot that it could do. She told her sister about how she teleported to Maine to try and find Grammy and

Grampy, and found herself in what she thought was the eighteen hundreds; but really it wasn't, they were just reenacting the civil war. She finished the story with the time travel that she just went on with Pete. Shelby began to laugh and told Abby that she was crazy. That's bull crap, Shelby said. Abby reminded Shelby, that you're the one who just saw me appear out of thin air, right? "Oh yeah", Shelby replied. "Ok Abby, I promise that I will not tell anyone about this magic phone". "It will be our secret, I promise you". Abby asked her to pinky promise, and Shelby gave her the secret pinky promise shake. Shelby then asked Abby if she could please go back to dad's sixth birthday again and take her along so that she could see this for herself. Abby replied that she thinks she can do it on her own now.

She took the phone out of her jewelry box, and pushed the start button. The phone detected her full hand contact and scanned her right fingerprints and opened up to the main page. She went into calendar and all of the previous information was saved. She told her sister to hold onto her hand really tight, because they were about to leave 2014.

Abby pushed the "Go To" tab and off they traveled back to their dad's sixth birthday party. When they arrived in San Diego, in 1969, Shelby could not believe what she was experiencing. She felt hypersensitive, anxious, and at the same time excited that this was actually happening. Abby called out to Shelby and she turned to her little sister. She looked at Abby's clothes and began to laugh! Look at what you are wearing, that is funny looking. Abby laughed and told Shelby "oh yeah, well you should see what you're wearing"! Shelby looked down and saw that she was wearing a short brown skirt with a leather belt, a shirt that was quite colorful with flowers all over it, sandals that laced up her ankle, a black armband, and a leather headband. They thought this was the funniest thing and they both laughed at how different they looked. As people were pulling up to go to the party, they watched these two girls going on about their outfits and laughing. They asked Mary and Gary who those girls were. They answered and said that they never saw those girls before, and didn't know who they were.

Abby and Shelby saw what was going on and that their grandparents were watching them. So, they walked away for a moment, and a few minutes later, Abby asked Shelby to walk across the street and to watch what was going on at dad's trailer. Abby told her sister that this is where dad lived when he was a young boy. Do you see those two adults over there, pointing to them? Those are your grandparents. The woman is Mary and the man is Gary, aka grandpa. Those are dad's mom and dad, our grandparents! More people began to arrive at the party. Shelby, keep your eyes on the front door, "really", Shelby exclaimed. Abby said, "just do it"! Within a few seconds, a girl walked out with the pitcher of Kool-aid. Abigail told Shelby that's aunt Brenda, and within a minute, their dad opened up the trailer door and jumped clear over the steps and onto the cement porch under the awning. He then took off to the back table where everyone was and began to play with his friends. The two girls watched their father on his sixth birthday and watched the excitement in their father's eyes.

They watched as everyone sang happy birthday to their father. This time Abby took Shelby by the hand and walked to the edge of the front yard. When their dad blew out his candles, he looked up at everyone with a big smile on his face and again glanced to the front of the yard. This time he saw two girls watching the party. Abby took Shelby by the hand and walked away from the party and hit the "Return Home" tab.

Within a second, the two were back in their bedroom. When the two girls looked at each other, they both said oh my gosh, at the same time! Shelby told Abby that that was incredible and thanked her for sharing that moment with her. Abby said you're welcome and then reminded her that she could not tell anyone. Abby said that if anyone found out, this secret magical device could be taken from me. Shelby told Abby, that she didn't have anything to worry about, that her secret was safe with her. Abigail began to describe what she saw while they were traveling back in time and when they came back. She asked Shelby if she saw all of the stars and space around them as they traveled back to 1969. Shelby said that she saw the same thing and that it looked like they were in a tunnel that was thin walled. She said that it was like a dark night, looking up at the stars. "You could see space all around you", Shelby said.

She began to describe the invisible thin shield that protects all of us from the harsh environment of space, our atmosphere. It's like the tunnel was a thin layer of atmosphere that protected us from space while we were traveling at the speed of light back in time. The two girls began to think how amazing that was and how amazing our earth is, that we are protected every day from the void of space by this thin layer of atmosphere, and that we are spinning around the sun, traveling through space as we speak. It's like we are on a space ship made of rock!

Chapter Six

Traveling to Philadelphia, 1776

At the moment that Abigail and Shelby traveled back in time, Pete received an alert on his phone. He knew exactly what date, time, and place they were traveling to and when they returned home. Pete had his phone set up as the master phone and Abby's as the slave phone so that anything that had to do with magic would push these notifications to his phone. Pete knew what was going on at all times and felt this was necessary to keep Abby, and anyone else that she was with, safe. Later, Pete received another alert that Shelby and Abby made it back home in about an hour and a half. He was pleased with Abby, and how she was beginning to understand and use the phone with the respect that it deserved. However, he was unsure of her sister, and felt that he would need to pay her a visit later on.

Later in the week, Abby remembered that she had to begin her book report for school. She wanted to write about the signing of the Declaration of Independence. So, she ran out to the kitchen to let her mom know that she was going to start her report for school. Her mom told her that if she needed any help, to just ask. Abby said, "thank you mom", and ran back into her room to start the report. As Abby began to write about the signing, she was also thinking about paying a little visit to the Continental Congress! After all, she remembered hearing her grandfather and mother talking about her 7th great grandfather, John Adams, and she knew that she was named after his wife Abigail Adams.

The wheels began to spin in her head. As Abby wrote more facts about the signing of the Declaration, and the conflicts that were occurring around Boston, and she began to write down dates that these events occurred. She wrote down the date that the declaration was signed and the address where it took place. She thought that it would be cool to take Mr. Adams for a little trip and show him what he had helped to create.

It took Abigail a little more than a week before she had completed her paper on the Declaration of Independence and she would need to present it in class in two days. Abby had her trip to Philadelphia all planned out in her head and began to make her reservations on the phone. She started by tapping on the clothing app, because she felt that she needed to have her clothing all in order before any arrangements have been made. She picked out a lovely dress, but was kind of disappointed with the selections that she had to choose from. She thought that she should give Pete a call and tell him that this App needed more work and that she could help him out with the clothing selection. She decided to save that for another day!

Once she had the dress, the only other two items she had to choose from were white stockings and black shoes. Abby did like the dress that she picked out; it was solid navy blue in color with a white shift. Now that she had the clothing, she opened up the Money App and selected the recommended allotment of money for a two-day visit. She laughed after she saw that she was only given a total of one dollar. She thought that if she bought dinner alone, that she would need at least fifteen dollars, plus a tip! Regardless, she closed the app out and opened up the calendar to put in the date, time, and place that she would arrive. She set the phone to arrive in Philadelphia at eight in the morning and that she was going to give herself seventy-two hours to automatically return, just in case she couldn't reach her phone or couldn't manually enter the return home tab. Once all of the information was entered, Abby noticed that the Go To tab was active in thc time travel section of the screen, and she also noticed two new areas that she had never seen before.

There were two small boxes that were checked off, clothing, and money. Abby thought, what a good idea, and said to herself "Way to go Pete"! Abby closed the phone after setting everything up and put the phone away into her jewelry box. She had planned on leaving after going to bed. When Abby walked out into the living room, her mother said that it was time to go to piano practice; so, she gathered up her music books and off they went.

Later in the evening, Abby helped her mother set the table for dinner and they had a chance to talk for a while. She wanted to learn more about her famous grandpa, and asked her mom to tell her as much as she could about him. Her mother told Abby that she could remember some stuff, but not a lot. She told Abby that John grew up in Massachusetts, just south of Boston, and lived on a farm. John wanted to be a farmer, but his dad wanted him to have a formal education. John's father was a deacon at a church, but by trade he was a farmer and a shoemaker in Braintree. She told Abby that John attended a preparatory school before going to Harvard at the early age of fifteen. He eventually became an attorney. Abby replied "Oh, and I remember hearing something about him defending a British soldier, after the soldier shot a townsman during a large gathering, who was protesting the presence of the British". Susan agreed with Abby saying "yes", and she stressed to Abby that he fought long and hard to become independent of British rule, while a member of the Continental Congress, and as you already know by your book report, he was a signer of the Declaration of Independence.

Abby smiled and told her mom that she was proud of her great grandpa. The family sat down to have dinner and later Abby read through her book report to make sure that she didn't make any spelling or grammatical mistakes. Her mom and dad came into her room at nine to tell her it was time to go to sleep. She gave them both a hug and kiss and her father sat next to her for a few minutes to talk about her day, and what she had learned in school. Once her father left her room, she got up and looked down the hallway to make sure the coast was clear. When she saw that it was, she pulled the phone out of her jewelry box. She put the sheets over her head and turned on the phone. The phone performed a scan, but did not see her fingerprints. Abby quietly said "Buttercup" and the phone opened up to the main screen. Abby then tapped on the calendar app. There it was, the active Go To tab! Abby was nervous with what she was about to do. She had never gone so far back in time and all by herself too! She was feeling a little scared, but she hit the button and like a wave, she was gone.

Abigail was no longer in her bed and time stood still in the present. She found her self in Philadelphia, back in the year of 1776. It was the morning of July 2nd and it felt hot to her already. She looked down at her dress and smiled. She liked how it looked. She lifted the dress high enough so that she could see her stockings and shoes. She liked the look, but told herself that it's time to find Independence Hall, "I am here on a mission"! Fashion will have to wait for a later date. Abby began to look around; she knew that she had selected a spot off the beaten path a few blocks away from Independence Hall. She was next to what looked like a tavern, but wasn't sure which way to go. So before going out onto the street, she pulled her phone out and opened up the Planet Earth App. She could see that she was on Chestnut, two blocks from Independence Hall.

She began to walk out onto the street and marveled at the people, their clothes, and the architecture of the buildings. Abby decided to stop at a stand where a gentleman was selling bread, fruits, and vegetables. She asked the man for an apple and a bottle of water. The man looked at her kind of oddly and told Abby that he has Apples for sale but not water in a bottle. She told the man that she would like the apple and gave him the coin she had. He gave her some change back, still shaking his head and mumbling water in a bottle? Abby was on her way, eating her apple and headed to Independence Hall.

Once she got to the Hall, she decided to sit on the steps so that she could see everyone walk in. Throughout the morning, she saw many men come into the building, most of whom she didn't know. However, she did recognize one person in particular. She saw him from about fifty feet away as he made his way to the building. Abby got a bit nervous and didn't know what she was going to say to him. As John approached the steps, Abby stood up and said "good morning Mr. Adams". He replied, saying good morning young lady. "Wow, what a beautiful dress you have on, I don't think I've ever seen such a beautiful blue color quite like that before". Abby said "thank you and actually a friend of mine made it for me". She then asked Mr. Adams if he had a busy day scheduled today. He laughed a bit and told her that he would be busy, and that he had some very important things to do for this fine country of ours. Abigail let him know, that if he needed anything today, to come out and she would get it for him. She said, "She would be his servant for the day"! He bent down to her level and said thank you, and by the way, what is your name? She said that my name is Abigail. He smiled and said that his wife's name is Abigail too. She smiled and acted surprised "Oh really, that is so cool"! He didn't know how to exactly respond back to Abby and asked her why she said that's so cool? Abby replied, "Oh, I meant that was very nice that your wife has the same name as me"; "I like that name"! Mr. Adams tapped Abby on the head and told her that if he needed anything, he would use her services. John walked into the building and very shortly thereafter the second continental congress was called into session.

Abigail went inside the building and hung out by the door to see if she could hear any of the debate. She took out her phone and set it by the door, tapping on the record button. As she did this, she made out a voice telling the rest of the men that we will read the declaration today and we must be diligent in it's wording. She could hear the declaration being read and she could not believe that she was actually there, listening in. Wow, this is so amazing she thought! Later on, she could hear an adjournment and the rustling of feet. She grabbed her phone and ran to the front steps of the building. As the men came out of the building, John saw Abby still on the steps and couldn't believe that she was actually still there, just like she said she would. He introduced her to a friend of his. Abby, this is Mr. Thomas Jefferson. Thomas, this is Abigail. She put her hand out and replied “very nice to meet you Mr. Jefferson” and Thomas shook Abigail’s hand. Wow, a smart and bright young lady you are. Where are you from, Thomas replied? She told him Long Island New York. His eyebrow rose a bit and he told her that he wasn’t very fond of New York at this point in time.

Abby asked why he didn’t like New York? So he began to explain that he doesn’t actually dislike New York, he’s just upset with their delegation in the congress. “In fact, I’ve been to Long Island a few times, to William Floyds home and it is a beautiful place, especially the beach”. “But, it is way out in the boonies, not much really out there”. Abby asked why he was so upset with New York? He replied by stating that twelve of the colonies have agreed to a resolution to adopt the Declaration of Independence from the British, except for one! She replied, “New York”? He nodded yes. Abby told both of the men, not to be upset by the New York delegates, that they will eventually come around. The two men looked at each other and began to laugh. Abby just smiled. John then told Abby that they had to leave for the day, and thanked her again for her offer of services. She told them good day and they walked off into the city.

Abby wasn’t ready to leave just yet, and settle in for the night. She decided to go to a Tavern and get something to eat and later to see some parts of Philadelphia that she learned about in her history book. She remembered hearing a story that her dad told her last fall about where the United States Marine Corps started, a tavern. She had to think about the name of the tavern. What was the name, Abby thought? While walking down the street, she remembered; it was Tun Tavern! Abby didn’t want to take her phone out of her pocket so she asked a gentleman where she could find Tun tavern? He pointed her down King Street and said that it is next to Tun alley. She made her way down King Street taking in all the sites and activities. She came up to what looked like a house with a front porch the width of the building. She thought this could be it and entered in. The place was mostly full of men who were drinking and talking.

The room grew somewhat silent when Abby entered the tavern. She felt awkward, but looked around for a table because she was really hungry. She thought about walking out and hiding somewhere. There, she could open the magic app and use the app for food and water. Just as she was turning to head out the door, a woman came up to Abby and smiled at her, asking if she would like to sit down and have some dinner? Abby smiled back, and said that she would love something to eat, that she only had an apple all day long, and could she have some water too? The woman said that would be just fine and sat her down at a table.

The woman came back with a glass of water and asked the little girl if she liked steak. Abby replied yes, I love steak! Great, the woman said, one steak coming up along with a potato and some vegetables from my friends garden. She then said that my name is Peggy, what is yours? "My name is Abigail". Peggy told Abigail that it was really nice to meet her and for her to stay here and relax for a while. She will personally get dinner for her. While Peggy walked off, Abby began to look around, and noticed some of the men who were at Independence Hall. She then saw Thomas along with John and a few other men, all sitting at a table in the corner. Thomas saw Abby sitting at the table by herself and nudged John and whispered in his ear. John turned to look around and saw

Abby sitting by herself. He got up and walked over to Abby's table, and asked if he could sit down with her. Abby smiled and said sure! You can sit down and have dinner with me. He laughed, and said that would actually be good and that he hadn't had anything to eat all day. Peggy walked up and said, "Oh, I see you have met Abigail, Mr. Adams", and he replied "why yes I have, I met her at the Hall earlier today". "Well, would you like to have dinner with Abigail"? John replied, "Peggy, I would love to have dinner with Abigail". She asked, the usual? He said that that would be fine. A few minutes later, Peggy brought them a few slices of bread. Abigail and John said thank you, and had a slice.

The two began to talk a bit and John asked Abigail, why she was here in Philadelphia. She told John that she was here to witness history in the making. What do you mean by that John replied? Well, rumor has it that you and other delegates should be signing the Declaration of Independence soon. He told Abby that he had hoped to sign it today, but it looks as though it should be passed within the next day or two. Abby told John that sounds great and that she agrees that as a country we should become independent, and that we should forge ahead with our own government and our own laws. He told Abigail that she was very smart for her age, and where she was going to school? Just then, Peggy came up with both Abigail's and John's dinner.

Abby asked John if she could say a prayer with him. He agreed and Abby reached over to hold his hand. John bowed his head down as Abby began to pray. She prayed for the leadership and the future of this country, and that the people of this country would bond together to make this a strong and good nation. She thanked God for the food we are about to receive and said Amen. Abby dug into her food, she was hungry. John laughed at the sight of Abby eating so fast and began to eat his dinner too. Abigail told John not to give in to the critics, and that what he's doing is a good thing for this country. After dinner, Peggy came by and asked Abby if she would like dessert and Abby said that she would love some. I love dessert she said. Abby asked if she had ice cream and Peggy said no, but had something special for her. Peggy came back with a bowl of bread pudding and said that this is on the house! Abby said thank you very much and began to eat her pudding. John said that he enjoyed dinner, but he needed to go home and write his wife a letter, and hoped to see her soon. He got up and paid for the two dinners and waved good-bye to Abigail.

Abigail left shortly after, thanking and hugging Peggy for all of her hospitality and Peggy told her that she was welcome, and to make it home safely. Abby left Tun tavern and made her way down the street. She found her way to a stable and crept slowly in through the doorway. She had a difficult time seeing once in the stable, so she turned on the light that came from the phone. Looking around, all that she could see were two horses and a few sheep. She found a blanket and laid it on the hay in a corner of the stable. Abby fell fast asleep.

Early the next morning, Abby felt breathing on her face, and very bad breath at best. She was afraid to open her eyes, but slowly opened one of them. She saw a horse's nose very close to her face and she smiled, petting the horse on his nose. The horse sneezed and walked away. Abby was grossed out after getting sneezed on by the horse, as she wiped her face off. It was time to get up, because she needed to get a move on. She saw fresh water in a large porcelain bowl and washed her face quickly and rubbed her teeth with her finger to clean them the best that she could. She then made it out to the street, and began her journey back to Independence Hall. On the way, she bought some fruit at the stand she stopped at the day before. The gentleman gave Abby a look of intrigue today.

Nevertheless, while walking up the street, she noticed a gathering where men were signing up to join the Marines and the Army. A man was telling the crowd that the war with the British has just begun and we cannot quit, we must win this war and become independent! "Independent from Tyranny"! Many men were signing up to fight for their freedom. Abby was inspired by their conviction and again couldn't believe that she was witnessing all this. Abby took a sheet of paper that a man was handing out, which looked like a recruitment advertisement for the Flying Camp Militia. Abby eventually made her way to Independence Hall and again waited for John Adams to show up. While looking over the street, Mr. Jefferson said good morning to Abby as he entered the building. She said "good morning Mr. Jefferson".

Many men were making their way into the building, talking to each other with determination in their voices. Abby noticed John coming up to the steps and she said, "good morning Mr. Adams, "I wish you the best today". He replied to Abby stating, "this should be a grand day" and thank you for your words of encouragement Abigail. She smiled at him and waved good-bye. When all of the men were in the hall, she peaked in through the keyhole of one of the doors and she could see the men gathering and ratifying the declaration. The men seemed quite intent on the exact wording of the declaration and the meeting lasted all morning and into the afternoon. At about 2:30 in the afternoon, John Adams came out and asked Abby if she could run to the market down the street and get him some bread for the men? Abby agreed and he gave her three cents. Abby ran down the street and bought ten loaves of bread. She ran it back and entered the room where all of the men were. She gave the bread to John and he was very thankful for it. "We are so hungry, Abigail"! Abby he said, it looks like we will be here for a while longer. Say a prayer for us that we can finish it today.

Abby walked out of the hall and went back to the market to get something to drink and eat for herself. She didn't want to go far from the hall so that she wouldn't miss out on seeing John after the meeting. At about seven, the men emerged from the hall and John came out looking tired, but he had a small grin on his face. She could hear John telling the reporters for the paper, that the Declaration has been completed and will be signed in tomorrow. John approached Abigail and asked where her parents were and where she was staying while in Philadelphia? She told Mr. Adams that her parents were still in New York and was given the opportunity to come to Philadelphia from a dear friend of the family and that she was staying at a hotel for the week.

He asked if she would like to accompany him for dinner, that there will be a large gathering at Mr. Jefferson's home. Abby replied to John saying that she would love to attend the dinner. So, they made there way down a few streets to Thomas' house. While on the way to dinner, Abigail told John that she wanted to share a few things with him and asked if they could sit and talk a for awhile. He agreed and they sat on a bench where they could watch the activity on the street, and discuss this important information from a charming young lady.

Abigail asked John to be opened minded while she talked to him. He agreed and asked Abby to continue on. Abby told John that the founding fathers, including him, had made a huge and positive impact on this country and that she has seen the positive effects of the work they have done. She said that she would like to show him a few things, but to be prepared for an amazing journey. He asked her where this journey would take them, that they didn't have much time before the dinner would start. She told John not to worry and to follow her.

They got up and Abby took John to the stable where she had slept the night before, so that no one was around. She pulled out the phone and told John that this is a device used for communication and to travel from one place to another and to even travel through time. If I show you how this works, you have got to promise not to tell anyone about it, not even your wife! He laughed a bit, and told Abby that he tells his wife everything. She said that she knows that, but that he cannot say a word about this. With reluctance, John agreed.

First, I am a granddaughter of yours of eight generations and I was named after your wife! Are you with me so far grandpa? He smiled and said, "I guess I am, but you do know, this is hard to believe". Abby told him that she could understand, but when you see what's about to happen you will believe! Ok, now about the device I'm holding. This button here will start the phone. John saw Abby push the button and Abby held it up to her eye. The phone scanned her eye and he was bewildered at the light that was emitted from this device. He stepped back, somewhat startled. She plugged in a time and coordinates of their travels with an automatic return time of 2 hours. She asked her great grandfather to hold her hand, that they were going to be transported to Washington D.C. He asked her why we would be going to that old swampy place? She told him, You'll find out soon enough, and whoosh they both were gone.

Within a second, the two of them were now in Washington D.C. next to a huge building. John asked Abby where they were and what is all this and why so many people? He then looked down and his clothing and asked, what in God's name am I wearing. Abby laughed and said that is a suite from the seventies. If you think that is bad, look what I'm wearing!! These pants are called bell-bottoms, not a pretty sight. They both laughed and then Abby told John that this is Washington D.C. and we are headed to a lawn at the Pentagon. What's the Pentagon, John replied?

Well, from what I know, Its a building where the military of the United states operates out of, but that doesn't really matter too much. For now, just follow me! She grabbed his hand again and took him to the lawn facing the Washington Monument, where they sat on the grass. She told John that the tall memorial was a monument for George Washington, our first president of the United States; it was lit up and looked stunning. She then showed him the Jefferson and Lincoln memorials as well. This is beautiful John exclaimed.

Abby then told John to watch out, that we were about to see fireworks shot up into the sky as a celebration to the signing of the declaration. He asked what date it was? Abby replied, "It's July 4th, 1976 and you are about to see the fruits of your labor". Americans celebrate this day from one end of the country to the other. We celebrate by bringing family together, having barbecues where we cook lots of food, we play games, and we shoot rockets and fireworks into the air. Just after she made that statement, the first of the fireworks shot off into the air. Abigail and John looked up into the sky admiring all the beauty. John could not believe what he was seeing and could not believe the impact that he and his peers have made for this country of ours. Abby looked over at John and smiled when she saw his face. He was looking into the sky in disbelief. Abby pointed out the capitol building, which she could see far off into the distance. The illuminations were beautiful against the Washington skyline. Time flies when you're having fun; Abby told John to hold her hand tightly, we've been here for two hours already, and within a few seconds, they were gone. No one around them even noticed, they were all looking up at the fireworks exploding over Washington D.C.

When they returned to Philadelphia, they walked out of the stable at the exact time they had left. They walked out onto the street and made their way to Mr. Jefferson's house for dinner. John stopped a few times on the way to dinner and shook his head in disbelief. Abby, I can't believe what I just saw. Abby told him, that he had better believe it, while smiling at the same time. They continued their walk and had dinner that night, where Abby got to meet many of the delegates to the second Continental Congress. One of the highlights of the night for Abby was when she asked John Hancock for his autograph. He told Abigail sure and she immediately pulled out the recruiting letter from a pocket in her dress. He took a pen sitting on Thomas' desk, and signed the paper for her in front of all to see. When he was done signing the document, everyone cheered, and

Abby smiled and lifted the paper into the air and shouted, “I have his John Hancock”! Everyone in the room began to laugh! What a great night this is Abby thought.

Later that night, Mr. Adams returned to his home in Philadelphia, and began a second letter that day to his wife Abigail. He wrote that the day of the signing of the Declaration of Independence would be memorable in the history of America. “I am apt to believe that it will be celebrated by succeeding generations, as the great anniversary festival. It ought to be solemnized with pomp, shows, games, sports, guns, bells, bonfires, and illuminations from one end of the continent to the other, from this time forward”. “You will think me transported with enthusiasm; but I am not. I am well aware of the toil, blood, and treasure that it will cost us to maintain this declaration and support and defend these states”. John folded the letter and placed it in an envelope to be sent out the next day.

Early morning, July 4th, 1776, Abby woke up after another night of sleeping in the stable. This time, she was awakened by the horse, which was licking her face. She stood up and needed to wash all that sliminess off of her face. She saw the ceramic bowl with plenty of water in it and freshened up a bit. She knew that this would be the day that all the delegates would sign the declaration! As she began her journey to Independence Hall, for the last time, she saw the man at the vegetable stand and said good morning to him. He said good morning and threw her an apple. Abby thanked him for the apple, and then he asked her if she would look at something for him. He stated that h he had been thinking of this idea for the past two days, and wanted to ask her what she thought. He lifted a canvas that covered a few boxes and he pulled out a bottle, telling

Abby that he had filled twelve bottles with the freshest drinking water in the area, and asked what she thought. Abby told him that this was a great idea and that it should be a big hit with everyone who's thirsty. She asked them gentleman, if she could take one with her to Independence Hall. He smiled and said sure you can have it; after all, it was really your idea. When Abby walked away, the man put up a sign that said "Bottle of fresh water for one Pence". The gentleman was on his way to expanding his business.

Abby had reached Independence Hall and began to say good morning to all the men who walked in. When John approached, she became excited just like the first time she saw him, except now she felt a love in her heart. After all, he was her great-grandfather, and plus, he was such a nice man. When he saw Abby, he became excited and ran up to her and gave her a hug; he thanked Abby for taking him on the trip last night and that he enjoyed every minute of it. I still don't understand how you did it all, but it was amazing. It's important that you know that I will do all I can for the best of this country; oh, and "I love you grand-daughter". They hugged on the steps of Independence Hall, but John had to go in now. Abby noticed John looking over his shoulder when he yelled out, "John, John Hancock, get over here, we will need your signature today, hurry on"! Abby told Mr. Hancock to make her proud. He smiled and said that he would do his best and patted her on the back as he walked by.

It wasn't long today before the men were on their way out the door. Abby ran to the front of the building and watched as they came out. All of the men seemed very happy, except for a few. She figured that one of them must be from New York, and rolled her eyes, as he walked by.

Then, Abigail saw John and asked him what happened, and he told her that 'John Hancock signed the declaration today, it is done'! The rest of us will sign an engrossed copy in a week or two. "Abby, A lot of hard work is ahead of us, men will die for our country, leaders will be born, and our nation will be strong"! John then asked when she would be returning home? Abby said that she is ready to leave now, and asked if John would walk with her. He told her that he would love to. They talked for a few minutes and John told Abby that he will never forget her, but will not be able to ever write about her.

She said that she understood, but would keep his words in her heart. Abby found an alley with no one in it. She told John that she needs to go home and waved good-bye, but then ran up to him, gave him one last hug and a kiss on his cheek. He pulled her in and gave her a loving hug and told her that he loved her very much. She told John that she loved him and that she was so proud of him. She stepped away from John, pulled out her phone, and with one tap, she was gone. John looked around, he couldn't see Abigail any longer, and felt a huge sadness come over him and empty, a tear began to run down his face when he realized she was really gone.

Abby was back in her bed in an instant; she pulled the covers down and looked around. She could see a light in the living room and she could hear the TV in the background. She got up and tip toed to the end of the hallway and saw her mom and dad watching television. She then slowly walked back to her bed, knowing that no time had passed since she left. She got back into bed and fell asleep very quickly. About an hour later, her father came into her room to check up on her. He got down on his knees and said a prayer thanking God for all that he provides, for his daughters and sons, his wife, and the beautiful pallet that he has created for us to see all around us. After his prayer, he stood up and went off to bed.

The next day, Abby finished her project on the signing of the Declaration of Independence, and a few days later, she gave such an enthusiastic presentation to her teacher and all of her classmates. She even took out a coin that was from 1776, along with the recruiting poster that was signed by the one and only John Hancock, and showed it to the class. The kids were really into her presentation and learned so much about the signing of the Declaration of Independence. Later, Abigail was given an A for her project, and told "good job" by her teacher. The, her teacher asked her if that recruiting poster was really signed by John Hancock, and Abby just smiled and said yep, that is his real signature. Her teacher could only say "wow, that is very cool Abigail". "I've never had anyone present their book report so well before". "Great Job"!

Chapter Seven

The Test of Integrity

Pete had decided to implement his plan to see if Shelby had the ability to keep an important secret, now that she knew about the phone. He had called over a few friends of his, who were in the business of security and counter intelligence. He knew them very well when he worked at the national laboratory and knew that they would be the men for the job. He gave them information on where they could find Shelby. Pete reminded them, that this was not going to be a real interrogation that this young lady is to be respected and treated well, but she needs to be tested. I have to make sure my technology is protected. The two gentlemen agreed and left's Pete's office to search for this girl and ask her a few questions.

Later that afternoon, the two men approached Shelby's house in their black SUV, and kept an eye on the front door to the house. After a short while, a bus stopped in front of her house, and she jumped off the bus. By the time she got to the front door she heard steps coming up behind her; she looked down at the key and contemplated putting the key into the door or spinning around and hitting whoever it was behind her with her forty pound book bag. She thought that if I hit them in the head it would take them out in one hit. Just before spinning around, she heard a voice, "Shelby, we are here to ask you a few questions".

Shelby turned around and looked up at the two gentlemen. One of them stated that he was agent Harding and the other said that he was agent Thompson, both showing her their ID and badges. Shelby noticed that they were both wearing a black suit, white shirt, and black tie. She thought, these guys look like FBI. Nevertheless, she asked if she could help them in someway. They told her that they would like to ask her a few questions. "About what" she replied? Well, we have information about a technology that can allow a person to do unbelievable things! Oh yeah, she replied. "What kind of things?

We feel that someone you may know owns a phone that can do things that most phones can't do. Shelby replied, "well, my brother has a phone that can talk to you and I've seen him put his phone up to a radio and it will tell him the name of the song that's playing". The agents slipped out a chuckle, but straightened up quickly. Young lady, this is serious and if you have any information on this phone we're talking about, we'd like your assistance in the matter. Other than that, I don't know what you guys are talking about, Shelby exclaimed.

Agent Thompson jumped in and asked Shelby if she recently traveled to California. She replied, "no I haven't". In fact, I've never been to California. He then asked her if her sister, Abigail, has a new phone. She stated that she does have a phone, but we all have one. Our parents want us to have one in case we need to get a hold of someone from the family. Agent Thompson was getting upset now and was ready to break this little girl. He then stated that we know your sister has a phone that can teleport you to anywhere in the world, and we know that you've seen it. Shelby began to laugh and said "Yeah right, beam me up Scotty" LOL. Agent Harding jumped back in to deescalate the conversation, and told Shelby that if she hears of anything that we are talking about, to please give us a call. He handed her a card with their information on it, and thanked her for her time. She said no problem, turned around and put the key in the door and walked inside her house. When she closed the door, she wiped the sweat off of her brow and breathed a sigh of relief. Soon after, the two agents reported back to Pete by phone and told him that Shelby got an A. She wouldn't give us any information and seems to be very trustworthy!

The next day, Shelby went to her father's house for the night and when she got home, she ran into her bedroom. She saw Abby and grabbed her by the shoulders and shook her a bit. Abby asked Shelby what was wrong. She told her that these men from the FBI came and visited her, and asked her all kinds of questions about your phone. She asked if they had approached her yet? Abigail said no, they haven't. Well, if they do, DO NOT tell them anything about your phone. Abby told her that she wouldn't "I promise". She then told Abby "you need to tell dad about this phone". He needs to know about it. Abby agreed and asked Shelby if it would be all right to talk to Pete first and then to dad.

Shelby told Abby that that sounds fair and that she wanted to meet Pete when she goes to visit him next. They both agreed that they would go visit Pete on Saturday, when Shelby was back for the weekend. Abby then called Pete to see if it was all right to visit with him and discuss a few things with the phone. Pete said that would be wonderful and that you're welcome anytime. Abby then asked if it would be all right if she brought her sister? He asked Abby if she was sure that she wanted to do that, or if she was being pressured to do that. Abby said that she wasn't being pressured and would like for her sister to be there. Pete agreed and told Abby to come over anytime in the morning.

On Saturday, Shelby was excited to take a walk over to Pete's house. Abby told her that we don't need to walk; we can shoot straight over there by using my phone. Shelby smiled and asked Abby "you mean that we are going to just teleport over there?" Abby shook her head and said "yep". Shelby and Abby went out to the kitchen and had breakfast with the family. They asked if they could go for a walk into Bellport this morning, and their dad replied yes, but to be careful and look both ways when crossing the roads. They agreed and when they were done with breakfast and cleaning up, they left the house.

Once they were about a block away and no one was around, Abby took out the phone, opened up the contacts and scrolled to Pete's name. She then tapped on his address, bringing up planet earth. She asked for Shelby's hand and tapped on the "Go To" tab. With a whoosh, they were gone and almost instantly at Pete's house. They knocked on the door and within a minute, Tillie answered. Tillie was excited to see Abby again and welcomed the girls in. Abby introduced her sister to Tillie and Tillie welcomed her to their home. She asked if they would like anything to drink or eat? The two girls asked if they could have some hot chocolate since it was getting colder outside. The weather had recently changed, the leaves were turning yellows, oranges, and reds on the trees, and it was getting a bit nippy out. Tillie said sure and went into the kitchen. While Tillie was taking care of the hot chocolate, she asked Abby how she was doing? Abby replied by saying that she was doing well and had a few opportunities to use the phone. Tillie smiled and asked if Shelby knew anything about the phone? Abigail said that she told Shelby about the phone and we went on an adventure together. She told Tillie, that after Pete and I went to see my dad's sixth birthday party, I took Shelby to see the same date and time. Tillie smiled and said that's great that the two of you were able to go back in time together and see your dad when he was so little! I bet you were in awe when you saw your dad for the first time as a kid! Both Shelby and Abby said "OMG" at the same time and they both laughed together. Shelby said that she couldn't believe it and Abby said that our dad was so little. He was so cute when he was a little boy!

Chapter Eight

Tillie's Adventure Back in Time

While the two girls were drinking their hot chocolate, Tillie told them, "Pete and I have been on a few trips ourselves". Would you like to hear one of my favorites, Tillie asked? Both of the girls drew close and said that they would love to hear a story. Tillie told the girls that her and Pete traveled back into time when she was eighteen years old. The cool thing about this story is that "I was actually eighteen years old. She told Abigail that she can't travel back into time any younger than she is now, that her phone isn't capable of traveling that way; but, at some point in time, Pete may upgrade your phone so that you're capable of doing it when you are much older.

Abby asked Tillie, "how that's even possible to travel through time and change your age". She told Abigail and Shelby that it's very hard to describe this, but would try based on what Pete had told her in the past. She took out a spiral notebook and opened up both the front and back covers. She drew the earth on both sides of the spiral. She then bent the front and back covers forward until they touched making a cylinder shaped object. She said that the front and rear covers represent space and the spiral is the divide to two parallel universes. If you had to travel through space from one end to another part or opposite end of space, it would take a long time.

Space is curved and to follow the curve it would take you forever to complete your journey. Now, if you can tunnel from earth through the center of the cylinder (space), you can arrive there a lot faster and go back in time. But, if you can find away to move through the spiral of this notebook, you are on the other side of the universe in no time at all. That's how you could go from now back to 1969 within minutes. Tillie said that there is one more thing we have to add to change your age while traveling back in time, and that's to travel down the spiral and out the other side at the right moment to get you where you want to be, at the right age. That took Pete and the people of Gmack awhile to perfect. Tillie also mentioned, to help the girls understand the spiral that as time passes, the universe travels in parallel to the spiral. If you move directly across the spiral, or dimensional plane, you will come out at the same age; but, if you travel up or down the spiral "dimensional plane" you will come out the other side a different age. The girls looked at each other with their jaws wide open. They were both blown away from what Tillie had just told them. Wow, Shelby said "That is so crazy". So, if you are seventy years old, you can move down the spiral and come out younger than when you left? Tillie said, "Yes, this is our fountain of youth". "Pete and I have been planning on a time to do this permanently, because we are getting pretty old now, and we want to be able to retain what we've learned over the years, but have younger bodies at the same time". Abigail and Shelby were excited to hear about Pete and Tillie's plans, and for them to be young again.

Just then, you could hear a door open up and the shuffling of feet coming towards the kitchen; it was Pete walking up from his basement laboratory. Pete saw the girls and with a big smile said hello. The girls got up and gave Pete a hug. He told them that they had grown so much since he had seen them last, and said that they were both so beautiful. Shelby and Abby thanked Pete for his kind words. They told him that he was looking pretty darn good too, as he kissed Tillie on the cheek. Shelby remembered meeting Pete a long time ago with her dad, and knew that these people weren't strangers. They had known her dad for many years.

Tillie told Pete that she was going to tell the girls about their trip back to 1958. Pete got all excited and told the girls that this was a cool story, and that he would like to tell parts of the story too, if that was alright. Tillie told him, "She would think about it", as the girls laughed out loud. He said "yes dear".

Tillie started telling the story to the girls. A few years back, Pete and I traveled to Bellport, and the year was 1958. When we lived in Bellport back then, Pete was actually twenty-five years old and I was twenty-four years old. So, we knew that there was a chance that we could bump into our older selves somewhere along our stay, but Pete had already graduated college and was working at Brookhaven Lab. In fact, I was working at the Laboratory by that time too. Before we went back into time, Pete made us driver's licenses that had our age on them and our new names. Pete came up with the name of Calvin for himself and I took the name Mary. We decided that I would be eighteen and Pete would be nineteen years old when we traveled back in time. When we arrived, it was sunny and warm outside, a great day to go swimming, they both thought. The date was June 21st, which is the longest day of the year, and usually pretty warm. Pete looked at Tillie and told her how beautiful she was. Her hair went from being short and grey to long and blonde. She was wearing Bermuda shorts with a white blouse, white socks and saddle shoes that were white with brown saddles.

He said that she was stunning! Tillie told Pete that you are looking mighty handsome yourself. She said that your hair is so dark. Pete was wearing a plaid shirt, straight leg Levi's with the cuffs rolled up, white socks, and penny loafers. Pete looked down at himself admiring his tight waist, something he hasn't had in quite some time, and the dapper clothes that he was wearing. He told Tillie "Hey, I'm looking pretty good if I say so myself". Tillie told him to "settle down big boy", and they began to walk down Main Street, holding hands, and reminiscing on how the town looked. They past the Ice cream shop on the right and then the grocery store on the corner.

They decided that they were going to check into the Bellport Inn first and get ready for a swim in the ocean. They entered the hotel, which was quite a fancy place. Pete commented that he never saw the inside of the hotel while he was growing up there; he had only seen it from the outside. After checking in, the bellhop took Pete's bag and helped them to the room. The room was up on the second floor, where they would have a great view of Main Street, allowing them the opportunity to watch the people in town. Tillie told the girls that Pete and I got our bathing suits on and headed down to Academy lane. At the end of Academy, was a great place to go swimming in the Great South Bay. Tillie said that we enjoyed the afternoon, feeling the sun on our bodies, the water all around us, and being able to jump around without hip or knee pain, laughing out loud. After our swim, we dried off and headed back into town. Tillie remembered seeing her mother coming out of the grocery store, and as she watched, her mother caught a glimpse of her and did a double take.

Tillie said that her whole body and mind was tingling, because she hadn't seen her mother in years. She stopped and watched her mother walk down the street. Her mother looking back at this person, she felt that she knew, but wasn't quite sure who she was. Pete smiled and asked if Tillie was ok. Tillie replied that she was all right, just a little overwhelmed right now. They continued on their way, back down Main Street; they walked past the clock at the corner of Main and station road. It was 12:30, and Pete asked Tillie if she remembered how the clock became old and finally broke down? Tillie, said that she remembered and that it was around 1978, when it broke.

As they continued down the street, Pete suggested that they eat at the diner and have one of their favorite dishes when they were teen-agers, a big cheeseburger with lettuce and tomato. Pete said that he liked mayonnaise on his and Tillie would have mustard on hers. Tillie said, "while we were eating, I could hear the door bell ring when the door opened", and I glanced back to see who it was. She immediately turned her head back around towards Pete, with this worried look on her face. It was her mother, but she had brought her father with her. The two of them walked past, and they were trying to get a closer look at us. She remembered her parents sat down at the counter, and began to whisper, looking back over at her. They bought a cup of coffee, while Pete and Tillie finished their cheeseburgers, but continued looking over at the two of them. Tillie told the girls, that her parent's then got up and walked up to her and asked, " we are so sorry for staring at times, but you look so familiar. Do we know you"? Tillie swallowed and said, "you look familiar too, but I don't know you. They asked her name and Tillie replied "Mary". They both shook their heads up and down and said “ohhhh”. Nervously, they said that they were Martha and Jim. Pete told them that his name was Calvin. They both told Calvin, that he reminded them of a scientist at the lab, named Pete. Nevertheless, Tillie got to talk with her parents for a little while, which made her trip back to 58 very enjoyable and a success!

Tillie said that they later walked over to Hawkin's Ice Cream Parlor and both had a black and white ice cream soda. Pete wanted the chocolate ice cream with vanilla syrup, and Tillie ordered the vanilla ice cream with the chocolate syrup. Tillie told the girls, "you know what they say, opposite's attract"! Pete really enjoyed his ice cream soda, one of his favorite deserts of all time. Tillie saw how much he was enjoying it and had to tell him that he better not eat too much of that, "you know that you have diabetes when you're older"! He said "yes dear", and kept eating every drop of his ice cream. In fact, he got up and ordered a small chocolate ice cream in a sugar cone.

He told the girls that "the ice cream cone was actually his favorite, and it was a weakness of his throughout his life". Tillie just shook her head in disbelief. Before sitting back down, Pete walked over to the Whirlitzer Jukebox to play a few songs. Abby asked Tillie, "what's a Whirlitzer jukebox"? She explained that it was a machine that had a lot of records in it, which played music. We would put a nickel in it and listen to our favorite songs. Tillie went on, saying that Pete put in a quarter and put in some of his favorite songs. The first song was by Elvis Presley. She said that Pete sat back in the booth and really startled her. She said that he pulled out a pack of Chesterfield cigarettes and lit one up. The girls both hit Pete on his arm and yelled at him "Pete, what's wrong with you"? “You cant smoke in a restaurant and plus it's bad for you", as Abby gave him the infamous evil eye! Pete laughed a bit and just said, "yeah, I know, but it was fun to do". Tillie said that it was really cool listening to the music that they loved in their early twenties. Pete surprised Tillie once more, when the song "Great Balls of Fire" started playing. Pete took her by the hand and led her to the middle of the ice cream shop and started dancing the Jive with her. The two were so amazed at how their young bodies moved so swiftly and quickly. Tillie told the girls, that Pete and I were having the time of our lives!

After dancing, the two of them relaxed at a table outside, under a shade tree, enjoying the summer weather, and time spent with someone that they really love. Pete then jumped in the conversation, and told the girls, "you wanna know what happened next"? They replied, "Yes"! Pete said that they met up with some of the other teenagers from Bellport, and they all planned on going to the drive in for a movie. The drive in was in the next town over, which was Shirley. Shirley, was a little further east on Long Island. Before heading out, Pete told everyone to hold up, and Pete, and one of the other guys, went into the grocery store and bought some beer and snacks. They loaded up the two cars, and headed to the drive in.

On the way to the movies, the guys began drinking the beer, and when they were done with one, they would throw the empty beer can out the window. Tillie then stepped in and told the girls, "Guess what happened next?" The girls didn't know, so they asked, "what happened?" "Well, Pete and the other guys got us pulled over by a police officer" They had thrown out a few beer cans right in front of his car. He happened to be parked off the side of the road, behind a sign. The police officer asked, "What in tarnation are you kids doing?" Pete was good at talking his way out of anything; so, he replied that they were just having a little fun and apologized for acting irresponsibly, and said that they would be good from here on out. The other guys chimed in and said, "We are sorry sir". The police officer warned them not to ever do that again, and they all promised that they wouldn't. The police officer then made the boys get out of the car and walk back to pick up those beer cans. After the cans were picked up, the kids were back off to the movies.

Just before they got there though, they pulled over and a few guys jumped out of the car and into the trunk, so that it wouldn't cost as much, and once in the drive in, someone would open up the trunk to let the boys out. Everyone got a big kick out of that. Tillie said that she actually had a few beers that night, and she usually doesn't like to drink beer, but we had such a good time. She went on to say, later that night, the boys acted up again and almost got caught again by the police. Tillie said that Pete and the boys went down to the Bellport dock and pushed someone's VW beetle from the parking lot to the end of the dock. The poor man, we could see him looking all over for his car later.

We watched the man get on a pay phone and call the police; we could hear him say that his car was stolen, on the phone. We all decided to head back into town and while walking up to Main Street we saw the police cruiser flying down the road with it's red bubble gum light spinning and the sirens a blasting. Pete and I said goodbye to the others and ran into the hotel. We couldn't believe that it was two in the morning, way past their usual bedtime of nine-thirty.

Tillie said that the next day was even better! She said "we took the train from Bellport into the city and headed over to Broadway for a play". It was very romantic sitting in the theatre, holding Pete's hand, and watching a play from 1958. Afterwards, we headed over to a restaurant that she loved as a kid. It was Horn and Hardart, an automat. She described the restaurant to the girls, stating that there were a lot of stainless steel doors with windows in them. There were labels up at the top describing the food in that particular set of doors. Once you found the food you wanted, you put in some coins and it would unlock the door and you could pull out the food.

Abigail and Shelby had never heard of such a restaurant where you would self-serve like that. Tillie said that she ordered her favorite as a kid, a BLT sandwich and tomato soup. Pete, on the other hand, said that he ordered meat loaf with mashed potatoes, green beans, and for desert, he bought chocolate pudding. Pete said "it was good too"! After dinner, they took a train over to Brooklyn to see her father's bakery that he owned. It was on Manhattan Avenue, Tillie said. She told the girls that in the winter, the sidewalks in front of his bakery never had ice or snow on them. The girls asked "how's that Tillie"? “Well, the level below the bakery is where the ovens were and the ovens were tucked under the sidewalks”. “So, the heat would radiate up and through the sidewalks, keeping them warm and ice free”.

Tillie also said, that in the winter, the bakery was a nice and warm place to be, but in the summers, not such a good place, because you would sweat ten pounds off in a week, laughing out loud. "That's how I stayed so skinny", Tillie said. Pete reminded her of one last stop before coming back home to 2011, "Remember going to the saloon?" Pete said that they headed over to Greenpoint Avenue, or was it Freeman Street"? Tillie said it was "Greenpoint". There we had a few drinks and listened to some music. Pete said that he got up and danced with Tillie during a few of the songs. Tillie told the girls "those were the good old days"! Well, enough about our stories. The girls thanked Tillie for her awesome story. Abigail told her that was awesome and that she hoped to do something similar when she gets older.

Chapter Nine

Should I Tell My Parents?

As Pete headed down to the laboratory, Tillie asked Abigail, "what is your favorite app on the phone? Abby told her so far, it's the calendar, because she was able to travel through time. She went on to tell her the story about meeting John Adams, back in 1776. Tillie listened to the story and was very impressed that Abby could do so much with the phone. Tillie told Abby, you're such a great learner and most importantly, you are a great listener; I've also heard that you are both very disciplined and have kept this secret to yourselves. Tillie warned them to keep this a very close secret, and to never tell anyone you don't trust.

Abby agreed and felt that this was a good opening for one of her questions. "Tillie, I feel that this is very overwhelming for me and I don't want to keep this away from my family anymore". "Should I tell my parents and brother about the phone?" Tillie told Abby that she was a good apple and that apple's don't fall far from the tree. That would make your parents good as well, since they are represented as the tree, and that by telling your mom and dad would be all right. You will just have to break them in slow to the idea of the magic phone. Tillie took the two empty cups of hot chocolate and walked them to the basement door. She told them that Pete is waiting for them down in his dungeon, laughing a bit, and said that they should talk to him. The two girls thanked Tillie and walked down into the laboratory, I mean dungeon, LOL.

As the girls descended the steps they could see Pete sitting at his workstation, working on the computer. They called out to Pete to let him know that they were coming down, and sorry for the lateness! I was telling Tillie the story of Philadelphia, and I went on about it too long. Pete said that was no problem and then asked why they wanted to meet today? Abigail began to explain to Pete, that Shelby and I feel that we need to tell our parents about the phone, because we are spending more time with it and that the FBI came by asking questions! Pete said, "Oh my, what did you guys tell them?" Shelby told Pete the story of them coming over to the house, but that she didn't tell them anything. Pete told them that was good that you didn't say anything. We don't want any Government to get a hold of this technology. They will take it away from us and use it for the wrong reasons.

Pete said that he understood the need to tell your parents. "Yeah, we don't like keeping things from them" exclaimed Abigail. I've felt bad about the sneaking around already, and what would we say if the police or FBI came by again? "That wouldn't be good", Abigail said. He told the girls that Tillie and I already know your mom and dad, and smiled. Shelby said "you know, I thought that I had met you years ago with our dad, but wan't sure". Well, we have known the two of them for about twelve years now, and they helped put us back together again, after our accident. See, a long time ago, we were in a bad automobile accident, because a teenager was texting and driving at the same time. She came across the median on the highway and hit us head on. I fractured my spine and Tillie broke ribs, and both her legs. In fact, I heard Tillie say to me "When I get out of this mess, I'm going to kick you in the butt". He laughed and said, "Yes Tillie".

When we got out of the hospital, we went to your parent's physical therapy facility where they worked on all of our injuries and gave us our lives back. You know, I actually met the two of you when you were very young, and Abby, I first met you when you were a little baby, we even baby sat you when you were real little. Your parent's have shown us pictures of the two of you and I recognized you Abby when you came into the store back in May. "Is that why you gave me the phone Pete"? "Well, that had a lot to do with it, but it's your good-hearted nature Abigail, that made me, even more, want to share my invention with you". "Abby, you are the light in a dark world". "Plus, I knew that I would be able to trust you and I've heard nothing but good stories about you from your parents and your teachers over the years".

"So, lets call your parents so that Tillie and I can meet with them to discuss the phone". "In fact, ask them to come over for lunch"! The girls began to laugh and they could feel the weight lifting off of their shoulders, knowing this would all be ok. Abby called her mom on the Magic phone and told her that they were over at Pete and Tillie's house, and that they wanted them to come over and have lunch. Her mother asked, "why they were over at Pete and Tillie's house?" Abby said to her mom that we met them awhile back, when in Bellport, and we've been having hot chocolate and talking with them this morning. Susan, asked Abby to hold on "let me get your father". When her mom got back on the phone, she told Abigail that they would be over in about a half an hour. Abby said that that would be ok and asked if they knew where they lived? Her mother said, "we know where they live!"

Abigail told Pete that they would be coming over in about a half hour. Pete said that would be great and asked the girls to walk up stairs with him so that he could let Tillie know. When, they all told Tillie, she said that lunch would be great. She then asked Pete to go into town and get a Pizza. Later, Abigail's mom, dad, and her brother Chad came over to the house. The two girls were a little concerned about what mom and dad would say to them, and were a little worried that they would be mad at them. When their parent's came into the house, Phillip and Susan gave Pete and Tillie a big hug and asked how they were doing? They said that they were doing very well, and have been having a great conversation with the girls. They chatted for a few minutes and then went into the kitchen for some pizza.

Pete began to discuss his career at the lab with everyone, he liked to tell old stories and everyone loved to listen to them too. As he continued, he began to talk about some of his accomplishments and inventions. Then, he began to tell them about the magic phone and some of the stuff that it could do. He then asked if they could keep a solemn secret if he discussed some of the advanced capabilities of the phone? The two of them looked and each other and they both shook their heads in agreement. Pete then looked over at Chad, with a stern look. Chad told Pete that he would keep this between him and his family only, "I promise". Phillip then reiterated to Chad that he wanted his vow of silence "nobody can hear or see anything about this phone! Chad replied and said that he will not tell anyone about the phone. "So, Pete, Tillie, and our family are the only people who know the existence of this phone?",

Phillip asked. Chad told everyone that he thought something was up, because Abby had a new phone for one and that he had never seen a phone like it. Plus, when I tried to access the phone, it zapped me and it felt like it blinded my eye for a while. They all laughed out loud. Phillip said that we would love to hear more about this phone Pete.

So, Pete continued on about the phone, now going into the deeper secrets of the phone. He told them that it could teleport you to other areas of the world, it could make changes in weather patterns, and that it can take you back into time or into the future. The phone has a medic application that can scan your body for medical issues, and cure many diseases, and heal injuries. Abby's parents were amazed at what Pete was saying. They weren't even second guessing him, because they knew of this man's achievements in science and his potential. Phillip asked Pete, "why are you telling us all of this Pete?"

Pete replied, "well, back in May, I met Abigail when she came into town. She walked into the phone store on a Saturday that I happened to be covering for my friend. She had Buttercup in hand and was looking for a phone. The sweet girl was interested in getting a phone, but didn't realize the costs involved with buying one and then setting it up on a network. I could tell that she was very embarrassed at that point and she began to apologize to me for wasting my time. Abigail again thanked me for my time and left the store. Pete said that he felt bad for her and wanted to change this girl's life and be able to do something which would make her happy.

Abigail said, "wait, I didn't leave your store without the phone"! Pete replied "yes you did, but you don't remember that". Abigail was bewildered. Pete went on " Abigail, when you left, I got on my magic phone and went back in time one hour". "I took my second phone to the trophy and awards store, down the street, and he engraved your name on the phone for me". "I told you that it was from a women who ordered it earlier, but it was really for you". "When I walked out of the engravers store, I saw you walking down the sidewalk with Buttercup and then you stopped to talk to a woman who was wearing a red dress and hat". "This gave me time to walk back down to the phone store and put your phone on the counter". "It wasn't five minutes later, when you walked back into the phone store". Pete had a grin on his face as he told the family this story. Abigail didn't know what to say, because she was beside herself.

"Then, I took her into the technician's room, where I have a lot of my electrical instrumentation and test equipment". "On the table, I had the two phones next to each other". "In fact, I had just updated them a few months earlier". "I've had a prototype that I tested for years, but these were my first generation phones, that were complete". "So, I offered one of the phones to Abigail and she accepted my gift". "She was so excited and very thankful; I told her that all the instructions were in the phone and that she could contact me anytime with questions or help".

"Now, Abigail has had this phone for five months already and she has used the phone with good skill". "However, both of the girls were worried and didn't't want to keep this secret from the two of you any longer". "So, they came over today to discuss how to approach the both of you on this tricky subject". Pete asked Phillip and Susan if it would be ok for Abby to keep her phone? The two of them agreed that it would be ok, and Phillip thanked Pete for the wonderful opportunity that he's giving Abigail, especially with all of the amazing things it can do. Pete began going over all the features with everyone. He asked Abby for the phone, and when he placed it into his hands, the phone scanned his fingerprints and access was automatically granted.

Abby was amazed that Pete could get into her phone. He was able to show everyone the most of the features on the phone. Pete then told Abigail that he wanted to set the phone up, so that your father has access too. She said that would be fine and wouldn't mind at all. Pete went through some advanced settings and opened up a security feature. He asked Phillip to hold the phone in his right hand and then he tapped an icon on the phone. The phone began to scan Phillip's fingerprints. He then asked Phillip to put the camera lens up to his eye. When he did this, the phone scanned the pupil of his eye. He told Phillip that he could gain access to the phone when needed. In the end, Pete let Abby know that she should talk with her parents before going on an adventure. That way they will be informed and you will be safer. It was getting late; so, Phillip asked if everyone would like to go out to and get some ice cream, one of his favorite things to do. They all agreed and had a great time in the wonderful company of friends and some good old fashioned ice cream.

Chapter Ten

Abby Helps a Friend

The next morning, Abigail woke up to the smell of eggs and pancakes. On Sunday's, her father would get up and begin to make breakfast for the family. She was excited and jumped out of bed and ran into the kitchen. She ran up to her dad and gave him a hug. He asked her how she slept, and she said fine. He asked Abby if she would like to make the scrambled eggs, "Sure" she said. Her dad got the eggs out of the refrigerator and a bowl to break the eggs into. Abby began breaking the eggs into the bowl, only spilling a little over the side. She then began to scramble them up in the bowl. Her dad turned on the stove to heat up the pan and he got the spatula out for her. He asked Abby to pour the eggs into the pan and slowly stir the eggs. She did this while her dad made the pancakes. Abigail woke up the rest of the family and asked them to get up, saying, "Breakfast is on". They all sat down at the table and had a great breakfast together.

Afterwards, Phillip cleaned up the kitchen, while everyone else began to prepare for church, and when they were all ready, they headed out. It was another beautiful day on Long Island, crisp and cool air, blue sky, and the fall foliage showing their colors in so many of the trees. The first thing Abby would do, while in church, is worship through singing, and Abigail would love to sing the songs at church. She would also sit in between her mom and dad, until bible study would start for the kids, usually after the songs.

Today however, she waited by the front door for a friend of the families to arrive. Abby knew that Anna would be coming up soon and would need help coming in, because she's in a wheelchair. When she saw her pulling up, she ran into the sanctuary to get her dad. He would help her out of the car and into her wheelchair. Once Anna was in the church, Abigail would push Anna into the sanctuary where she would have a great view of the pastor as he spoke.

She helped her out of her coat and went back up to her mom and dad. Soon, Abby was off to bible study learning more about Gods plan. After the sermon, everyone would come into another area of the church to have coffee, tea, and bagels, and to catch up with each other. Abby stood next to Anna and asked her if she wanted anything this morning? Anna said that she would love to have a plain bagel with cream cheese on it. Abby then ran off to get her the bagel. When she returned, the family talked for a while and invited Anna back to the house for the afternoon and dinner later on.

Abby was excited to hear that Anna would be joining them for the afternoon, and helped her dad transfer Anna in and out of the car. After wheeling Anna into the house, Abby asked her how she was feeling? Anna said that she was doing just fine. Abby knew that Anna was in an accident about 15 years ago, which caused a spinal cord injury, but didn't know much more about her injury and why she's in a wheelchair. So, Abby just kind of looked at her for a little while. Anna asked, "What's going on in that head of yours Abby"? She told Anna that she loved her very much, and asked her why she has to be in a wheelchair all of the time? Abby said that she would love to see her stand up and walk again! Anna told Abigail that when she was in the accident, her spinal cord was injured. She went on to say that the spinal cord is just like a bundle of wires that sends all the messages from the brain to the rest of your body, and in the accident it was severed into two halves at a level between the shoulder blades.

Since the accident, the brain cannot communicate any longer with my legs and I cannot stand up or walk anymore. Abigail felt so bad for Anna and wished that she could walk again. Abby asked if there was a cure for a spinal cord injury? Anna told her that there is not a cure for this kind of injury. She said that physical therapy keeps her arms strong and her legs stretched out, which allows her as much freedom as possible, but that she is still restricted to the wheelchair. About that time, the rest of the family came into the living room and asked if they would like to play a game? Anna said that she would love to and asked if they could play a few card games. The family spent a few hours playing cards, and had a great time with Anna. After the games, Abigail went back into her room and took her phone out. She opened up the MDF and in the search field typed in "spinal cord injury". Nothing for spinal cord injury came up, but the MDF referenced her to the Time Search engine on the phone. She clicked on the hyperlink and it brought her to a section of the MDF that discussed how to use the built in search engine "Gateway". 3.0 – Gateway browser and the "Time Search" Engine:

Abigail closed the MDF app and opened up Gateway. She typed in spinal cord injury treatments and hit the enter key. Within three seconds, a list of treatments came up for this type of injury. She clicked on a link from a hospital located in the Washington D.C. area and read about the advancement of a treatment that completely regenerated the neural tissue within the cord. She continued to read about the breakthrough and treatment approaches. The website discussed the use of stem cell treatment to fix the spinal cord and that was now the easy part of the treatment.

The difficult part was getting the muscles that haven't been used for a long time, and are very weak, to tolerate long durations of physical therapy and rehab. The doctor's recommended that the earlier the treatment the better the outcome. Abby thought that she needs to get Anna to the doctor's, but in 2038, when the treatment has been perfected! How can I do this, she thought? Abby began typing in notes on her phone and initiating a plan of action. She would find away! Her mother called her in for dinner, so she put her phone away and ran into the dinning room. During dinner, Abby would look over at Anna and she would think about how she would love to help out such a sweet woman and make her all better again.

Abigail didn't have a lot of time to research her project because of school, piano practice, dance, and homework of course, but after school she would get back on the phone and search different categories via the Gateway browser. She was curious and began typing in her family names. Abby's jaw dropped once again. She found out that her sister was a veterinarian and living in the Raleigh North Carolina area. When she typed in her brother's name, she saw that he was a "What"? A doctor!! This is the same guy who is always playing around and not serious about anything? She couldn't believe it. He was an orthopedic surgeon at a large hospital outside of Raleigh.

She then looked up information on herself. When the search results came up, it was blank. A message came up and it said “This search request cannot be completed, Abigail, you cannot access your own name”. Abby typed in her big brother’s name and found out that he owned a company that created websites in the downtown Raleigh area. Abby thought, “This is a cool feature”!

A few weeks had past and Abigail was off of school for the holidays. Now that she had more time to research her upcoming mission, she began the finalizing stages, but there were logistics that would be hard to accomplish. She had to think about how she would get Anna into see the doctor, admitted to the hospital, create an ID for her, etc… She didn’t know how to do this kind of stuff. She began to think. Eventually, Abby decided that she would get her mother involved, because she always took her to the doctors office when she was sick, right? She would know how to take care of the same for Anna. Plus, her mom was Anna’s best friend and she would want to be a part of this.

So, she ran out of her room and began to discuss this with her mother. She asked her mom if she would like to help out a friend? Her mom said “yes”, but who? She said Anna. Susan, then asked Abby what do you have planned to help out Anna? I found a treatment for a spinal cord injury and it would make Anna all better again. Susan asked Abby for more information, because she knew there currently wasn’t a repair for that type of injury. Abby said that the treatment is available at a Hospital in Baltimore and that she would be able to get the money for the procedure, she thought. She said that she would need to check with Pete on that one. But, if she could get the money, she would need her mom to set up the appointments for Anna. "The only thing, Mom, is that we need to travel into the future to the year 2038"!

Susan asked, "you want me to travel twenty five years into the future"? And Abigail said "Yep!" Susan asked Abby to show her the research that she's gathered so far. When Abby was done showing her the research, her mother agreed to help out. Susan stated that the next step is to let Anna in on the mission, but we can't let her in on our secret! So, Susan gave Anna a call and asked that they meet soon. They decided on a day later in the week, where they would meet for lunch. Susan began to discuss some of the details, with Abby, that must be kept secret. She told Abby that when we do this, we need to wait until Anna is a sleep, and then bring her to Baltimore. We also need to go into the future and make the arrangements for her doctor's appointment and hospital visit. Abby told her mom that she knows what Chad is going to be when he grows up! And then Abby paused. Well, are you going to tell me her mother asked? He's an orthopedic surgeon in Raleigh. He may be able to help us out if we visit him first. Susan said, "That might not be a bad idea". Abby and her mother continued planning for the trip until they met up with Anna.

A few days had past and both Abby and her mother were on their way to meet up with Anna. They were going to take her to one of their favorite places to eat, Cafe Gia. They got to her house and wheeled her out to the minivan and began the drive to the restaurant. For the most part, they kept the talk very general. During lunch, Susan asked Anna if they could discuss something important with her, and Anna said of course, "what is it"? Susan, being a physical therapist for many years, said that Abby and I have been researching spinal cord injuries and treatment approaches that could completely cure your injury. Once the procedure is done, we let you rest for a month or so, and at that point we should notice trace muscle contractions in your legs. Once we see this, we begin rehab for neuromuscular reeducation, strengthening, balance, and learning how to walk all over again. Anna didn't know what to say, she hadn't heard anything about a treatment for her condition, and she had researched it for at least a year. Susan told Anna that we have taken care of all the finances through fundraisers and the surgery will be of no charge to her. All we need to do is get you to see the doctor and schedule you for the surgery. "What do you think?" Anna began to cry because this was a miracle coming true.

She told Susan and Abby that she has been praying that one day she would be able to stand up from this wheelchair and walk away from it forever. She told the two of them that she would love to do this and thanked them for taking the time to put this all together for her. Anna asked, "When would we be doing this"? Susan said that she needs to meet with the doctor first and then we will make the appointment for you to see him. Also, this procedure is not available to most people and is not an approved procedure by the FDA yet. It's still in the research stages, but it has been effective on many patients. If you want to go through with this Anna, you have to keep everything we do a secret. You can't discuss the doctor's name, where he's from, or how you were healed to anyone. Susan told Anna, that the doctor could get in trouble if we tell anyone that he did this procedure. Anna agreed! It was very hard for Anna to finish her lunch and she had to wrap it up and take it home for later.

After they dropped off Anna, Susan told Abby "we need to meet up with Chad in the future and talk with him about this procedure". They both began to laugh, "oh my word, can you imagine meeting Chad twenty five years from now"? Abby said, "That would be so cool." When they got home, Abby took out the phone and began to research where Chad lived, where he worked and the dates that he worked as a surgeon. They found out that he just turned forty years old in the year 2038. Susan told Abigail that we would pay him a visit this weekend. We also need to talk to Pete about getting enough money for the surgical procedure. By the end of the next day, Abby had talked with Pete and he said that he would upload$200,000 in our trip account. Abigail asked her mom when they should arrive to meet Chad? Her mother told her to get the phone and let's check on the date. Abby got the phone and opened up her calendar; she scrolled to the year and her mom said that we should meet him on a Saturday, when he will be home.

They picked November 20th, 2038. Abby went to the bottom part of the calendar app "Time Travel" where she tapped the select date tab. The date wheel came up and she selected the year, month, day, and then the time of 10:30am. Once this was done, she inserted a default limit of twelve hours to return home. The next field to do is the destination. Abby tapped on this field and the calendar app disappeared into the phone and the Planet Earth app came out of the black hole that the calendar disappeared into. Very cool feature Abby thought. She went to the search field and put in the address where her brother was living, an address in Wake forest. When she tapped the location on the map a blue cross began to glow.

Her mom told her not to go to his house that we have to arrive somewhere close by. "We can't let his family see us like this". So Abby moved the cursor around and found a large building in a shopping plaza about three miles away. Once the location was selected, She tapped on the done tab and was sent back to the calendar. She showed her mom how the "Go To" tab was now active. After she picked the date, they went to the clothing app to select clothing for the time period. What was cool about this part was that the clothing they were wearing now was a similar trend twenty-five years into the future, how convenient. Abby picked out her clothes, but there was no way for her mom to pick out her clothes.

Susan was just a little disappointed not knowing what she would be wearing. Abby said "OK" we have the phone ready for the trip this weekend. Susan called Chad into the living room and had him sit down. She began to explain to him that there will come a day when you will be visited at least one time in the future by myself and Abby. Chad said "for real?" and shortly after said "that's cool, I look forward to you two visiting with me". Seriously, if that happens, you will know what's going on ahead of time and not to freak out. She also told Chad to always keep his phone number, you never know, we may need to call you some time. Chad said "No problem". "Wait, it sounds like you guys have something planned already". Susan said that "we do have a trip planned and it will happen, just after you turn forty years old, but don't worry about that, just be expecting us".

By the time the weekend came around, Abby was so excited and couldn't wait to take her mom on this trip. She ran into her bedroom and saw that her dad was still sleeping. She went around into the bathroom where her mother was. She saw her mom sitting on the floor, leaning back against the drawers, and she seemed upset about something. Abby asked her what was wrong? Susan told Abby that nothing is wrong "I'm just a little scared to be so far away from home and I don't want to get lost somewhere, and we can't get back home. Susan began to cry and Abby sat in her lap and gave her a hug. She told her mother that everything will be fine and not to worry, and she held that hug until her mom stopped crying. Abby wiped away her mom's tears and Susan said "it's time to do this for Anna"!

They got up off the floor and Susan went over to the bed and gave her husband a kiss on the cheek and said that they would be gone for just a little while. They walked into the living room together and Abby opened up the calendar app. She held her moms hand and looked up at her. Her mom was closing her eyes as tight as she could, anticipating and fearing the unexpected. Abby said "here we go mom, hold on tight!" Susan held onto Abby's hand, Abby tapped on the go to tab, and with a whoosh, they were gone.

Susan opened her eyes for a moment and could see the universe all around her and it appeared the only thing in-between her and Abby and space was a thin layer that formed a tunnel. She got the sensation that they were traveling fast, but not from inertia, just a visual sensation, and within another second Susan and Abby found themselves next to a building. They looked at each other and Susan began jumping up and down, excited that she was on the ground and they were both alive! Abby saw that her mom was excited; so, she began to jump up and down to celebrate with her mom. At this point, a family in a minivan drove buy watching these two people jumping up and down screaming next to a Lowes store.

When they saw that they were being watched, they stopped jumping up and down and Susan pulled out her cell phone and went to call Chad. For some reason, the phone call was not going thru. She looked down at her phone and it indicated "No Service". "Oh my gosh Abby, my phone is not working"! Abby was shaking her hand and looking at it. Her hand was quite red and her fingers were squished and she saw an imprint of her mom's ring on one of her fingers. Her mom had squeezed her hand so hard when they traveled through time that it hurt. Abby told her mom that her phone is too old and won't work anymore. "My gosh, your 4G phone is three generations old now mom". "I'll call Chad with my phone mom."

Abby dialed Chad's number and handed the phone to her mom. Susan gets on the phone and waits for Chad to answer. After the third ring, a man answers the phone, "Hello" with a deeper voice than she is used to. Susan said "hi Chad, how are you?" Chad replied "hi mom, I'm doing fine, how are you?" "Oh, I'm doing fine I guess" "Are you Ok", Chad asked? Susan said that she was fine and asked if he wouldn't mind picking up Abby and I from the Lowes down the road. He asked "what happened to your car and why are you at Lowes"? "Where's dad"? She said, "Dad was at home and just to come pick us up, now, and not to bring anyone with you".

When Chad drove up, his jaw dropped and then his mind went back twenty-five years ago, when his mom told him that we might be visiting you in the future. He got out of the car and bent down to give his sister, who was a mere ten years old, a hug, and then he gave his mom a hug too. "Holy cow" Chad said. "I can't believe you guys are here, what's going on?" Susan told Chad that we are going to bring Anna to a Hospital in Baltimore to see a doctor. We are going to have him treat her spinal cord injury. Chad thought for a minute and said, "I thought that she was cured already"? I remember her being cured along time ago. "Don't you remember mom"? "Remember when you spent about eight months with her in physical therapy?" His mother was looking at him funny, like she had no idea what he was talking about. Then, Chad realized that they don't know, because it hasn't taken place yet. So, Chad said, "that he would love to help and asked what he could do"?

Well, we were thinking that you could contact the doctor and get us in to see him for Anna, and then he could schedule a time to perform the procedure. Also, let him know that your dad and I are physical therapists and we will be doing the rehab for her personally. Susan pulled out a piece of paper and gave it to Chad. She told Chad that this is the doctor's information. We will come back in a month to see you and check on your progress. Hopefully, you will have an appointment for us, Susan said. Chad said that he would have it taken care of in no time. Abby gave her big brother a hug and said that we will see you very soon. Chad hugged both of them and they backed up about ten feet. Susan looked down at Abby and nodded her head that it was ok to go back home. Abby took her phone out and opened it; she took her mom's hand and held onto it tightly. Abby tapped the return tab and with a whoosh, they were gone.

When they got home, in the living room, Abby opened the calendar app and slid the date wheel ahead one month to Saturday, December 25th. Abby looked up at her mom and told her to hold on, we are going back, and on Christmas day! Her mother closed her eyes tightly and held onto Abby's hand just as tight. They arrived back at the same location, except this time it was lightly snowing. Abby gave Chad a call and asked him if he could stop by Lowes again to talk with mom and I? He told Abigail "Do you know that it's Christmas"? "Yes, we know that it's Christmas"!! Chad told her that he would be right up. Chad told his wife and the kids that he would be right back. He has to meet mom and Abby for a little while. When Chad arrived, his sister and mom looked cold. He had them get in the car, where it would be warm and they could talk. They asked Chad what he was able to do with the doctor. He told the two of them that he called the doctor and introduced himself and that he would like to meet him at his earliest convenience. Chad invited him to his country club for a round of golf and they could discuss his idea at that time. The doctor agreed to meet for the golf outing the next weekend.

Chad stated "During our conversation, I mentioned that we have a family friend, from another country, who had a spinal cord injury several years ago and we wanted to have you perform the surgery for us". She is not a U.S. citizen and doesn't have insurance, but we have raised enough money for the surgery. After an hour of discussing the case, the doctor agreed. He said the best thing to do is bring her into the emergency room on a day that he is covering and he would do it as an emergency procedure.

Chad pulled out his phone and gave them the dates that he would be on call at the hospital. The three of them agreed on a date in January to arrive at the hospital. Susan told Chad that she is so proud of him for helping us out. He said that it was no problem and would be there the day of the surgery. Chad asked if he could get back home to his family so that the kids could finish opening up their presents? They all started to laugh and Abby said sure, that's the least we could do. Just then, Chad's phone rang. He looked at the phone and said that it was his wife. When he answered, his wife asked him where he was. He said with mom and Abigail over by the Lowes store.

His wife said “that’s funny, your mom just came over with presents for us and the kids”! Chad told her that he would be home in five minutes and he would explain. When Chad got off the phone, he told his mom that you just came by the house with gifts! “Oh man, I’m in deep trouble”! Abigail and Susan looked at each other and said “oops”, and started to laugh. Susan and Abby reached over and gave Chad a kiss and wished him a Merry Christmas. The two of them got out of the car and within seconds, they were gone. Chad looked around for them, but couldn’t see much because the snow had begun to fall harder.

Susan and Abby were home in a flash! Susan was glad to be back home. She walked out of the living room and into the bedroom, where Phillip was and saw that he was still sleeping. Time had not changed here at home. Susan then went over to Chad’s room and then Shelby’s, where they were both still sleeping. Once Susan knew that everything was OK at home, she met Abby in the kitchen and discussed about talking with Anna soon. Susan began to make breakfast and the smell of French toast baked with apples and cinnamon woke everyone up. The whole family had breakfast together, and Susan was pleased. After all, she had just been through a lot this morning and was happy to be back home with her family.

Later in the week, Abby and Susan gave Anna a call and told her that everything has been set up. Susan asked Anna “when can you get away to do this”? “You will need to be away from home for about a week”. Anna said that she would be ready in a few days. She told Susan that she wants to get her suitcase out and get her clothes and bath things together for the trip. Susan said that that would be fine. We will pick you up and you can spend the night with us prior to the trip. Anna said that would be great and thanked her again for all that she has done! When Susan got off of the phone, she let Abigail know that we will be doing this in two days. The plan will be to bring Anna over and she will spend the night with us. While she is sleeping, we will transport her to the hospital so that she doesn't know that we are traveling through time. She can't know that! You need to let Chad know that we will be at the hospital at 5:30am and we will meet him in the southwest corner of the parking lot by the tree line. Also, let him know that we will need a wheelchair and blankets to keep her warm.

Abby said "Yes Mam" and saluted her mother. Abby pulled out her phone and said that she would be right back. Her mom said "ok, see you soon" and turned around to wash the dishes. Abby went back to wake Forest in January of 2039. She sent Chad a text letting him know when we would be at the hospital and the things to bring. She got a text back from him saying "no problem, see you soon". Once she got the confirmation from Chad, she returned home. Susan turned around and saw Abigail standing there. She asked "I thought you were going to tell Chad about the arrangements"? Abby told her that she already did it. Susan just laughed and shook her head.

Two days had past and the family picked up Anna and was driving her to their house. Anna was excited and talking about how she looked forward to the day of standing up and walking away from this wheel chair. She began to talk about all of the things she hoped to do. She said that she would like to be able to get up and walk to the bathroom on her own, to have easier access into stores, the bank, and to be able to go grocery shopping all by herself again. Anna had the biggest smile on her face as she dreamed of these freedoms she may have again! When they got home, Susan and Abby set up Anna's bed for her and told her that they would leave early in the morning. Anna reached out to Abby and Susan, and held their hands, and said that she trusts what they are doing and is so appreciative. The two of them hugged Anna and they were excited about all of this as well. After dinner, they helped Anna into bed, and gave her a sleeping pill to help her get rest, and then said "good night".

Once Anna was in bed, Abby began to plan the trip on the Magic Phone. She put in the date, time, and place, right in the southwest corner of the parking lot at the hospital. She set the default return time to ninety-six hours, because she wasn't sure how long the surgery and recovery would take. She confirmed all of this with her mom and the trip was a go! About an hour later, Susan quietly walked into Anna's room and saw that she was sound a sleep. They sat Anna up on the side of the bed in between them; it was hard to keep her upright because she was sleeping and tilting from side to side. They started to laugh a little, but were trying to be quiet too. They were able to stand her up and stabilize her long enough for Abby to quickly get the phone and hit the "Go To" button.

With a whoosh, they were headed to Baltimore. Susan and Abby were able to hold Anna without any problem while in the time tunnel, but as soon as they arrived, Anna got real heavy. Chad saw them arrive and wheeled the chair over real quick and just in time, because Anna was falling back and right into the wheel chair. Chad put the blankets on her so that she would stay warm. Susan told Abby that she liked her jacket that she was now wearing. Abby then realized that the magic phone picked out her clothes and jacket for her. She had forgot to put in a clothing selection so the phone did it for her, "nice" she said. They wheeled Anna up to the emergency department and told the receptionist that their friend had an accident and is unconscious. Chad told them that he is an orthopedic surgeon and he feels that she has a spinal cord injury and to get the neurosurgeon ASAP! They called the doctor and he was down within a few minutes. He took it from there.

Anna was wheeled into an operation room. The doctor told Chad and his mother that everything will be ok. I'm going to take some images of the damage and begin the treatment; I should be out in a four to five hours. The three of them looked at each other, with a sense of relief, as she was taken into the operating room. Chad took his mom and sister out to his car and told them that he had reserved a hotel room for them so that they would be able to get something to eat and have a place to stay while in town.

Chad told them that the doctor would text him updates as he could, and that he would relay those messages back to them, as soon as he got them. Later that day, Chad got a message that the surgery was a success and that he expected a full recovery. He outlined a plan of care for the incision, proper time intervals for positioning, and the rehabilitation timeline.

He said that the physical therapy is very important to regain her range of motion, strength, and functional independence. He told Chad that Anna could leave the hospital in two days. Chad thanked him so much for his expertise and kindness and told him that he would call him soon for another game of golf. Chad then relayed the message to his mom and Abby that Anna was doing well.

The next day, Abby and Susan went to the hospital to visit Anna. When they walked into the room, Anna was sitting up in bed eating breakfast. Abby shouted out "Anna"! "How are you"? Anna turned to Abby and told her that she was doing well and the doctor said that I would be fine. Anna said that the doctor was just in about an hour ago and said that I'm healing well and I should start to feel movement in my legs in about a month. Susan and Abby were excited to hear the good news. They spent the day talking and playing a few card games that Abby loved to play. When visiting hours were over, Susan let Anna know that they would be back tomorrow and would be taking her home soon.

The next day, the three hung out in Anna's room keeping her company and talking about all the things that she will be able to do soon. Anna told them how excited she will be when she stands up for the first time. The nurse came in several times to check up on Anna, and on this occasion, Susan asked if she could be moved to a wheel chair so that we could take her to the cafeteria for dinner and take her to the patient lounge? At that time, the doctor came in and did an evaluation on Anna. Afterwards, he said that she is ready to go home and he will begin the paperwork to discharge her from the hospital, and that it's ok for her to transfer from the bed to a wheelchair now. When the doctor left, the nurse and Susan helped transfer Anna to a wheel chair. In two hours, they were able to leave the hospital.

Susan contacted an ambulette service to drive them to the hotel where they could spend their last night in Baltimore. When Anna went to sleep, Susan and Abby began their trip back to 2013. Abby and Susan held onto both sides of Anna, this time lying on the bed, when Abby tapped the return home tab. They ended up back in Abby's bedroom lying on the floor, and the two of them said, "That was much easier than trying to stand her up". They got Anna up and tucked her into bed. After Anna was tucked in, Abby said, "Mission accomplished".

Anna stayed with the family for a week to take care of her incision sight, and shortly after, she began her long duration of physical therapy. Within a month, the muscles in her legs were beginning to contract and her strength began to improve quickly. At the three-month period, after the surgery, Anna stood up on her own and walked ten feet for the first time in over three years! Everyone in the physical therapy department stood up and began to cheer! Susan was standing at the ten-foot mark and took her into her arms for a big hug. All Anna could do was laugh, out of pure excitement and then she began to cry from happiness. On the one year anniversary of the procedure, Anna, and her family went to Florida for vacation where she was able to walk for days through several theme parks. She even got to take a walk on the beach and feel the sand and water running around her feet and in between her toes.

Chapter Eleven

Learning New Things

Abigail was excited to hear about all the progress that Anna had made and she was so happy to be able to help out such a close friend. Abby thought that this would be a great way to use the powers from her magic phone, by helping others, if she could. It was a cold rainy day in February and she didn't have much to do so she decided to go into the MDF to learn more about her phone and what it was capable of doing. Abby thought it was kind of funny that she had this phone for about ten months now and that she's only used a few of the functions, but learning and doing so much at the same time. When she accessed the MDF, she began reading through many of the chapters.

She read about the weather app in section 4.0 and how it can manipulate the weather, "Oh my, I can't believe this phone can do this! Oh, and in section 6.0, she began to learn about the Magic wand app., which would allow her to fly, lift heavy things up into the air, push them and pull them around as if they weighed nothing. Unreal, she thought, it has a laser that has three intensities, which can cause some major damage, a shield to protect me, and flight school, which can teach me how to fly safely. This is awesome stuff, she thought. Abigail continued reading through the entire MDF. Before going to bed, Abigail opened up the clothing app and ordered the Magic pack. She wanted a new backpack anyway. Within a second, the Magic pack was sitting next to her on the bed. It felt so light when she picked it up. To Abby, it felt so light that if she pulled on it, it would probably rip. So, she pulled on it, tugged, and tried to tear the material, but it stayed together and it maintained its shape too.

She took out her old backpack and pulled her homework and books from it to the Magic pack. She noticed the inside lining was made out of a light flexible metallic material. Abby thought "one last thing"! She took her phone and opened up the Food & Water app. She scrolled to the snack selections, and then scrolled down through the selections. She saw one of her favorite snacks of all time, chocolate chip cookies. So, she ordered those cookies. Within a few seconds, she saw some movement in her Magic pack. She began to zip it open and looked down into the bag; she smiled and pulled out the package. It had five of the nicest looking chocolate chip cookies that she has ever seen. They looked so good.

Abigail knew it was time to go to bed, but had to try one of them. She pulled one of the cookies out of the pack and took a small bite. She began to eat it slowly and rolled it around her tongue to get a good taste. Next thing you know, she got that little smile on her face again, and took a big bite out of that cookie. Wow, was that delicious, she thought. She ate it slowly so that it would melt in her mouth and last longer. Abby closed the package and put it back in her Magic pack. It was getting late at night, so Abby decided to go to bed and get some rest. She thought that it would be best to read through the MDF one more time tomorrow and start practicing using some of these features. Abigail fell off to sleep very fast; after all, she was tired and overwhelmed by all of this new stuff that she had learned today.

The next day was a school day, so she couldn't hang out at home and read all that the phone was capable of. Abby got ready for school, grabbed her Magic pack and headed out to the bus stop. Abigail was so excited to have her new backpack with her. Abby enjoyed going to school, loved learning and didn't like to miss a day, unless she was really sick of course. At lunch, she met her friend Vanessa and they sat together, as they usually do, and while they ate their lunches, they talked about their weekend; then, the conversation turned to two boys that they kinda liked.

Abby said that she liked a boy named Steven and said that he was cute and very nice to her. She also said that she caught him staring at her lately, and knew that he liked her. Vanessa knew him and said that he will be outside after lunch, and we can go talk to him if you want. She then went on to say, that she liked a guy named Mike, who is in the sixth grade. She said that he's dreamy, smart, and very polite. She said that he asked me out to the movies, but I don't think that I can go with him. Vanessa said that her parents probably wouldn't let her go by herself. Abigail told Vanessa that she should ask her parents because it never hurts to ask, and they may say yes! Vanessa smiled and said that was a good idea and would ask, because she really wanted to go on her first date with him.

After lunch, the girls went outside to the playground. They got on the swings together and started going faster and higher with each push, a competition these two girls had with each other. The girls were going so high you could see that they were actually going higher than the top pole of the swing set. They could feel that weird feeling in their stomachs when they dropped out of the sky when heading backward on the swing. The girls were laughing and having a great time. Abigail yelled over to Vanessa and said, "ok, lets run over to the monkey bars and hang upside down". They both jumped off the swings and Vanessa flew through the air further than she usually would, landing on her feet, but falling onto her right knee. She scrapped her knee up pretty badly and it started to bleed.

Instead of going over to the monkey bars, Abby walked Vanessa over to a small area over by the trees, where none of the other kids were. Vanessa was gasping in air almost as if she were going to cry, but holding short of actually crying. Abby took a look at her knee and told her that it would be ok. Vanessa said that she would need to see the nurse now and began to cry. Abby told her to hold on for a second, stating, "I can help". Abby pulled her phone out and opened up the Medic app. She held it up to Vanessa's knee and began a scan of the scrape.

The phone instructed Abby that the knee would need to be disinfected and to tap on the disinfect tab and keep the laser pointed at the injured area. Abby did this and the phone began to scan over the entire knee. After about thirty seconds the scan stopped. The phone began a second scan and then informed Abby that the wound was clean. The next set of instructions told Abby to pull out the dressing from her Magic pack and to cover the wound to prevent future infection. Abby had left her back pack inside the school building, but would take Vanessa in with her and cover up her wound.

As Abby looked up, Vanessa's eyes were wide open, and looking right back at Abby. She asked Abby what was going on and what is your phone doing to my knee? Abby said that it was a new app that she just downloaded from the App store last week. Abby thought "oh no, she can't let Vanessa in on her secret and what this phone can do". Abby thought for a second and remembered to open the camera and take a picture of Vanessa. So, Abby opened up the camera on her phone and turned the selector wheel to erase. She told Vanessa to smile, that she wanted to take a special moment photograph. Vanessa smiled and pointed to her knee. Abby took the photo, with the camera emitting a brighter than usual flash, and for a few seconds afterwards, Vanessa looked a little stunned.

Abby looked down at Vanessa's knee and could tell that it had already started to heal. Vanessa asked Abby what happened. She told her that she fell on her knee but it looks like it will be fine. Abby suggested that they go in now and she told Vanessa that I'll cover up that little scrape with wrap so that it will feel better. They both went inside to Abby's classroom and Abby pulled out her Magic pack. She unzipped it and sure enough!!! The dressing for Vanessa's knee was there. Abby opened it up and wrapped her knee. She said, "see, it's all better now", and gave Vanessa a big smile. Vanessa said thank you and gave her best friend a hug before running off to class.

The next day, Abigail met Vanessa at lunch and the first thing that she noticed was that Vanessa was not wearing the bandage any longer, and that her knee had no scrape, sore, or scab on it. Abby was amazed at how well the Medic app worked. Abby asked Vanessa how her knee felt. She said that it feels fine and that she didn't really remember how it even happened. "That's cool" Abby said. After lunch, they went outside to play. Of course, the first thing they did was run out to the swing set and swing as high as they could, but this time no one got hurt.

Afterwards, the two girls saw Steve over by the school hanging out with a few other boys. They decided to go over and see what the boys were doing. Steve became very shy when Abby stepped up to the group of guys. He asked her how she was doing and Abby replied, "I'm doing all right, how about you"? Steve said "good". Abby looked over at Vanessa and smiled and of course, Vanessa smiled back. Abby asked if they would like to meet up after school today and play some softball at the field. The guys said sure, they would love to do that. Abby leaned over to Steve and asked him if he could get Mike to play too, because Vanessa likes him. Steve said sure, that wouldn't be no problem.

That afternoon, all of Abigail's friends and a few more kids came out to the field to play softball. Abigail got to play on Steve's team along with Vanessa and Mike. Abby's only experience of playing softball was with her father and her two brothers. They taught her how to throw the ball, hit the ball with a bat, and catch, but she never actually went around the bases or played a position. She asked Steve if he wouldn't mind helping her out, because she never played before. He was so excited to show her all about softball. After all, he played little league for the past six years and was a resident expert.

The team got together and talked about the positions they would play and he put Abby on second base. Steve would play on the pitcher's mound, Mike in the outfield, and Vanessa was at first base. The rest of the team went to the other bases, shortstop, outfield, and the catcher's position. In the first inning, Abby's team started in the field. Abby was having a hard time playing her position, when the first line drive, that was hit, went right between her legs so fast. The second batter came up and hit the ball right back to the pitcher, for the first out. During the inning, the ball was hit towards Abby a few times, and each time she either couldn't catch it or the ball was hit so hard that she couldn't react fast enough to get to the ball on time. A few of the players began to gravitate closer to her, just to help out. After awhile, Abby's team was able to get three outs. The first three players, on her team, had came up to bat and two of them got onto base. Now, it was Steve's turn to bat. He came up to the plate looking like a pro already. The pitch came towards him and Whack, the ball went all the way to the fence and bounced off of it. Steve could run so fast, which allowed him to make an infield home run!

When Abby got up to bat for the first time, she was able to hit the ball, but couldn't hit the ball very hard. The ground ball went straight to the short stop as she started her run for first; she was running as fast as she could, but was thrown out at first base. Abby laughed it off and her team mates told her "good job", although it wasn't really a god job, Abby thought. Abby needed to turn it up a little bit and pulled out her phone. She opened up the speed control and slid the control slide to the right by one click. She thought, "This should speed me up just a bit".

The score was three to three at this point, when her team went back into the outfield; that's when Abby tapped the start tab of the speed control. She could feel a difference instantly. She could hear voices around her, but they seemed a little slow and slurred. Her friends were moving around the field slowly. Abby noticed the ball moving at a slower pace too when Steve pitched the ball. It was just like everything was moving in slow motion. On the next pitch, the batter hit the ball and went off towards the short stop. He picked up the ground ball and threw it to first base for an out. Abby couldn't believe how slow everything was moving. Now, the second batter came up to the plate and Steve pitched the ball. The first swing was a hit and it went straight to Abby at lightning speed (real time). She put her glove up and waited a few seconds for that slow ball to move right into her glove. The team cheered Abby for making such a hard catch look so easy.

The next batter came up and hit the ball out in between right and center field. Abby watched the ball heading up into the sky; so, she started running back to catch the ball. In real time, she beat both the outfielders and caught the ball. Again, everyone cheered for Abby. Steve ran up to Abigail and told her "way to go out there Abby". She turned the speed control to the off position, so that she wouldn't appear odd, because of the speed at which she was moving compared to everyone else, and told him "no problem, it was nothing".

The first time Abby was up to bat, she turned the speed control back on. She walked up to the plate very slowly so that no one would notice her moving too fast. When she got up to the plate, she did a few practice swings, trying to move a little slower than normal so she wouldn't draw too much attention to herself. The first pitch came towards the plate and it was heading for the ground; so, Abby didn't swing at the wild pitch. The second pitch was thrown too high, but the next ball was coming right towards the plate. The ball appeared to be coming at her at such a slow speed. Abby had to wait for the ball to get to the plate, and when it did, she smacked that ball with as much speed as she could muster up. The bat must have swung at over a hundred miles an hour. The bat made contact with that slow moving ball and whack, over the fence it went. Abby watched the ball head over the fence and she started running around the bases. Abby forgot about her speed and ran the bases at a very fast pace, according to everyone watching her. It looked like watching a movie that was sped up a little bit. Abby's team ended up winning the game, fourteen to three, which was stopped by the lack of light on the field, now that it was getting pretty dark. So, all the kids ran off to make it home in time for dinner. Abby had a great day and really enjoyed playing outside after school, which is something she doesn't really get to do that often.

Later that week, and after all of her schoolwork was done, of course, Abby took out her phone. She wanted to try a few new things from the Magic Wand application that looked really cool. She remembered seeing the part about moving objects around, and flying too. Abby knew that she would need a private area to practice using this particular app in her phone, and one of the most desolate areas on Long Island is out on the east end. So, she decided to travel to one of the farms out east on the Island. She set up the Magic phone and teleported to the north fork of Long Island, right in the middle of a large field. She made her way to an area that had a few farm items.

Abigail saw a large irrigation pipe being held up by large metal wheels, a tractor with a disc harrow attached, an old pick up truck, and a tiller. She opened up the app and began her first command, which was "lift". She pointed the magic phone at the old pickup truck and could see that she was locked onto it through the viewfinder. She commanded it to lift, and directed her hands upward slowly. The truck began to tremble and shake. Dirt and dust became unsettled and began to fall off of the truck, and then it began to lift off of the ground. Abby was exerting no effort while doing this, but she did notice that the phone was getting a little warmer. She then voiced the command "Down" along with a downward direction of her arms, and the truck settled back down on the ground.

Then, Abby locked onto the tractor and commanded, "Pull". She began to pull the tractor towards her. However, the tractor must have been in gear, because the tires were dragging through the dirt as it was being pulled. She then commanded, "Push" and pushed the tractor away from her again dragging the back tires across the dirt. Just as she stopped pushing the tractor, a farmer came up and was looking around to see what was going on. He asked who she was and if she heard any unusual noises? She said "hi mister" and that she didn't hear anything unusual. Then, the farmer saw the marks on the ground where the tires were dragged across the ground. As he was looking down at the ground, he asked Abby why she was out here on his farm, and at the same time kneeled down to look at these drag marks a little closer. He didn't hear a response from the little girl; so, he asked her again why she was out here on his farm, and why there were tire tracks around his tractor. Not hearing anything from the girl, he turned back towards her, looked around, but Abby was nowhere to be found.

Within an instant, Abby was back in her room. She got out of there just before the farmer could ask her any more questions. Her heart was racing, because she felt that she was about to get caught doing something she shouldn't be doing. Abby went out to the kitchen where her dad and Shelby were. Abby asked her dad what he was doing. He said that he was making a peanut butter sandwich for lunch and asked if she wanted one too? Abby said that would be great. She asked her dad, who loves you? "You" he replied, and who do you love? "You"! They both smiled and her dad handed her a sandwich. The three of them sat down at the table to eat and her dad asked her what she was up to?

Abby told her dad and Shelby what she had just done, and was experimenting with the phone. Her dad didn't know that the phone had the powers to move and lift things like that. Abby told him that you could even fly with it. She said that she wants to go to flight school soon. She told him that the Magic phone has a tutorial to learn how to fly safely. Phillip told her that was really cool, and he would like to watch her when she was learning. She said that would be fine, stating "I would prefer someone to be there with me, so that I'm not alone". When they were done with their sandwiches, her dad asked her to come out to the garage with him. He said that he needed some help with a new project. Abby said “sure”, and they headed out to the garage.

He told Abby that he needed to put the engine and transmission into his new 289 FIA Cobra, an old school race car, and since my engine lift isn't here right now, maybe she could lift the engine and drop it into the car for him. She said that she would try. Phillip and Shelby covered the front fenders with soft blankets, so that nothing would mess up the paint on the car. He told Abby that this was the engine that’s going in and that we need to get it into the engine compartment. Her dad said that he didn't know how this would go, but that he would help guide it into place over the motor mounts.

Phillip gave her the ok and Abby opened up the Magic Wand app. She gave the command to lift, pointing the phone at the engine and transmission. She could see that the phone was locked onto the engine. Abigail gave the command to lift and the engine began to lift as Abby slowly lifted her arms up. Phillip was blown away by this and couldn't believe that this was actually happening. Once the engine was about three feet in the air, he told Abby to hold there. He asked her to push the engine back a little bit. Abby said the command "push" and the engine went back slowly. Her dad pushed down on the back of the transmission to guide the unit down into the car and then asked Abby to slowly lower the engine down. Abby then said "down" and very slowly began to lower her arm. As the engine and transmission slowly lowered, her father guided them to there exact location, right on top of the engine mounts.

Phillip and Shelby tightened up the four bolts for both engine mounts and the engine was now secure into its new home. Phillip turned around towards Abby and said, "Wow, I can't believe you did that"! She smiled at her dad and shrugged her shoulders stating, "no problemo". Abby asked her dad, "since I helped you, can I invite a friend over so that we can play out back"? Her dad said "sure, no problemo". So, Abby went inside to call her friend and her dad and Shelby continued putting his race car together.

The next day, Phillip let Susan know that after church, Abby and I would be going to the beach for some father daughter time. She said that was fine, because she would be going to the mall for some shopping. Phillip said “that's great, just don't spend too much”, with a smile. That afternoon, Phillip and Abby headed out to the beach. While driving out there, Abby began to read the MDF again, to make sure she knew what to do. The MDF hyperlinked her to the flight training program. The flight training would take her step by step through various modes of training, starting with the easiest of maneuvers to the most difficult maneuvers. Abby had her magic earring in so that she could communicate with the phone better.

Once they reached the beach, they decided to walk to a remote location where nobody would be watching, and during the winter season, there weren't many people out on the beach anyway. Abby showed her dad, that the first command would be to lift up slowly and land slowly. The Magic phone instructed her to give the command "Fly" and to slowly lift her arms slightly. So, she gave the phone the command to "fly" and began to lift her arms up slowly. She began to levitate and she felt off balance, wavering from side to side, and fore and aft. While about five feet up in the air, and several minutes of flight time, she began to regain her balance.

However, every time she moved a little bit, she would feel a loss of balance once again. Once Abigail felt oriented, she looked down at her dad and began to move forward, so she quickly moved her head back up to stop her forward movement. The flight school program then asked Abby to move her arms up and down slowly to get used to moving up and down. The program then asked her to move her arms more quickly to increase acceleration. Abby lifted her arms up quickly and kept them there for about five seconds, a little longer than the flight school program asked her to do, and by the time she could react and bring her arms down, she was about one-thousand feet up in the air.

The phone began to give her flight information, on speed and altitude, stating "your speed is approaching one-hundred miles an hour and your altitude is one-thousand feet". Abby's instinct was to drop her arms down to her sides, which she did, again avoiding what the program was instructing her to do, and she fell at a high rate of speed towards the ground. Luckily, there is a built in altimeter feature that will automatically decrease her descent so that she will land somewhat softly, and this feature kicked in, allowing Abby a slow landing. When she hit the ground, she fell onto her bottom. She thought the landing was a little rougher than what was described in the flight program.

Abby's dad asked her if she was ok, and she told him "that was a crazy ride"! He told her that he was a bit nervous watching her move so quickly up and down and suggested that she move her arms up and down a little slower next time. Abby's dad helped her up and she tried it all over again. Shortly, she was flying with more fluidity, and beginning to feel her way around this flying thing. The flight instructor then asked Abby to flex forward at her waist so that she could begin to experience forward flight. Abby did this and began to fly forward at about a forty-five degree angle upward. Then the flight instructor asked her to slowly raise her arms up, which will increase her speed. She did this and as her speed increased quite rapidly and she flexed slightly more with her trunk and her flight orientation changed to more of a horizontal position to the ground.

The program then instructed her to slowly lower her arms, which will slow her down and bring her back to a forty-five degree angle and at the same time extend her trunk back slightly to bring her back into a vertical position, preparing her for a landing. Abby continued though this flight school for about an hour and learned a lot. She learned how to turn while in flight, turn without speed, and fly at higher altitudes. After about two hours, she was ready to take a break and go home. She knew that she would need to keep practicing to get really good at it, and told her dad that she would practice as much as she could.

Abby asked her dad to give it a try. She told him that you used to be a pilot and you may be able to do it better than me. Abby handed the Magic phone to her dad and she instructed him to give the command fly and gave him a briefing on how arm movements will effect his flight. He told the Magic phone "fly" and with a slow upward movement of his arms, he began to elevate. Her father had a pretty good understanding of flight and did fairly well. He slowly raised his arms up and tilted his trunk forward, moving into forward flight. As he extended his trunk back and kept his arms half way up, he began to fly upward. He moved his right arm up higher allowing him to turn to the left and fly back towards Abby. He lowered his arms to slow his speed and extended his trunk back to bring him back into a vertical position. Then, he lowered his arms all the way to make a soft landing. Once on the ground, he told Abigail that that was a rush and thanked her for allowing him to experience flying like that.

Within a few weeks, Abigail's skills improved to where she could fly higher, further, and with much better coordination. The flying became second nature and so much more fluid that she was able to maneuver like a fighter jet.

Chapter Twelve

Spring Break

The winter on Long Island had dragged on for quite some time and most of the people who lived in the north and northeast of the United States were tired of the cold temperatures and snow. From Minneapolis to New York, the weather was frigid and record snowfall amounts were being recorded. For Abby and the kids, Spring break was just around the corner, and all the kids were hoping for good weather during this week off. During this last week of school, the kids could since that Spring break was getting very close, and Friday would be their last day before the break.

Abby was walking through the hallway, going to her next class, when she saw one her friends being picked on by one of the biggest bullies in the school. Him and a few of his friends from the football team liked to mess with the smaller kids and scare them. Abby even witnessed the bullies taking money from other kids, in the past. Abby watched as the bully pulled John's hat over his head and then spun him around about ten times, causing him to get real dizzy. Then, the bully stopped the spinning with John facing away from him and he grabbed the back of his underwear and pulled them up, giving John the biggest wedgey she had ever seen.

All the kids began laughing at John and you could hear John begin to cry underneath his winter hat. That wasn't enough for the bully; he had to start pushing on John. Abby instinctively pulled out her phone and opened up the Magic Wand App. She pointed the phone at the bully, but down by her waist, so no one could see what she was doing, and commanded push. Just as her friend John began to push back against the bully, so that it looked like John threw the bully ten feet down the hall way. Abby's jaw dropped when she saw that the phone was able to throw the bully that far. All of the onlookers let out an "ohhhhh", and began to laugh at the bully. John pulled up his hat slowly and looked to see where the bully was, and he saw him on the ground, lying on his back, ten feet down the hallway.

The bully's friends ran over to him and helped him up, but he pushed them away, and then told John that he better watch out, that he was going to get him later. Abby walked over to John and told him that he was cool for standing up for himself. She also said "I wished someone were here to help you out too, like a teacher". He told Abby, "That would have been helpful". Then, John said, "I don't even know what happened"? She told him that he pushed the bully so hard that he flew right down the hallway.

As they began to walk to their class, the students opened up the hallway so that he could pass between all of them. They were showing their respect for standing up to the biggest bully in the school. As they passed, many of the other students were patting him on the back, giving him high fives, and making comments like "Way to go, that was awesome dude, and you rock man"!

Before the kids knew it, the school week was at its end and the last bell rang. All of the kids were excited and began heading down the hallways for the buses. Abby and John were walking down the hallway when Abby noticed the bullies down at the other end. She could tell that they were looking for someone and she figured that they were going to mess with John one more time before spring break. She told John that if that bully picks on you again "I bet you could grab his shirt and lift him off the ground"! He said, "I don't think so". Before you knew it, the bullies were right up on John and they told him that he was going to get hurt today. Abby whispered to John and walked away.

The boys started to push John around from one boy to another. This continued for about a minute, and just before the big bully cocked back to hit John, John grabbed him and attempted to lift him up, and to his surprise, the bully's feet levitated from the ground. John had this look on his face like he was superman; everyone seemed to freeze when they saw the bully being lifted by John. He then threw the bully up against the wall, where he fell to the ground, and then John turned to the other boys. They looked at each other for a second and they all decided to run away. Everyone in the hallway began clapping and cheering on John. He just smiled and continued towards the bus with Abby, like nothing had happened. After all, John wasn’t a boastful guy, he was more of a humble kid.

On Saturday, Abby woke up and ran over to Shelby's bed to wake her up. She shook her and told her to wake up. Shelby began to grumble a little bit, but Abby persisted until she was awake. She told Shelby that it was spring break and we can't waste it by sleeping all day. Shelby asked her what she wanted to do? As Abby looked outside the bedroom window, she replied that she wanted to go to the beach and build a sand castle and jump into the waves at Smith Pointe. She said that there are big waves at Smith Pointe! However, Abby began to notice the gray sky as she looked up from her window. Her smile turned to a disappointed look and she told Shelby that it was cloudy outside and it didn't look like a good beach day. Shelby got her phone out to check the weather and told Abby good luck going to the beach; it's going to be 45 degrees today with a sixty percent chance of showers. Abby started to pout and walked into the kitchen where mom and dad were eating breakfast.

Abby grabbed the oatmeal and hot water pot to make her breakfast. She told her parents that she wanted to go to the beach today, but the weather still stinks outside. They told her that it wasn't going to be a good beach day and maybe they could start out spring break by going to see a movie. Abby smiled and said that sounds good; after all, we have to make the best of the situation. As she ate breakfast with the family, they began to talk about the things that they would like to do this week. Dad said that he would like to go out in the garage and continue building his race car. Abby's mom said that she would like to go to Paris for spring break. Shelby and Chad said that they both would like to go to the beach and hang out with their friends. Abby said that she wanted to go to the beach, but would also like to visit grammy and grandpa up in Maine.

Later that day, the family drove up to the theatre. After they got the tickets, Abby asked if she could get some popcorn and a soda. Dad said sure and walked over to the concessions stand and bought the kids each a small bag of popcorn and a soda. When they got into the theatre, Abby started to look at her phone while slowly munching on her popcorn. Abby opened up the weather app and looked down at the screen. Again, disappointed when she saw the cold temperature and cloudy all day. But then, her eyes opened wide and she realized that she could change the weather. She had forgotten that the app could actually allow her to change the weather. She thought, "I am so forgetful"! "This phone does so much, I can't remember it all". So, as the family began watching the beginning trailer, Abby tapped on the change weather tab. She selected the current location, a high pressure for the weather pattern, and then slid the temperature scale over to 80 degrees; once this was done, she tapped the confirm tab. At that time her father told her to put her phone away, because it was distracting. She asked her dad that if it's sunny after the movie, could we go to the beach? After seeing the weather report this morning, her dad smiled and said sure Abby, we can go to the beach, knowing good and well it would be cloudy and a bit on the cold side today.

After the movie, everyone walked outside the theatre and they all began to look up at the sky, as if something strange were happening. They were all squinting and looking at how bright the sun was and a man commented on how blue the sky is. Phillip said, "not only is it sunny, but it's warm too". Abby, acting like she didn't know what was going on went along with everyone and said that she could not believe the weather was so nice all of a sudden. Her father looked down at her and said "Abby, do you have something to do with this"? She just shrugged her shoulders and smiled, and then he said, "I guess we're going to the beach, right"? And Abby said "Yep".

So, the family went home and gathered all of the beach stuff out of the garage, the buckets, shovels, cooler, and umbrella. Then, they ran inside to find their bathing suits and off they went for the first day at the beach for the season. As mom and dad laid in their lounge chairs soaking up the sun, the kids were off running down the beach. Chad started skim boarding and you could see Abby slowly moving into the water that was still very cold. Shelby was on her phone texting her friends and posting some beach pictures on one of her apps. It wasn't more than twenty minutes before Abby was back, so that she could get a towel around her to dry off. Her lips were slightly blue and she was shivering, but it didn't take long for the sun to warm her back up.

Later, the kids played in the sand and built a few sand castles. Then, Chad buried his feet and legs up to his knees, into the sand, and laid back on a towel. He asked the girls to carve out two lower legs from the sand, which made it look like he was lying out flat on his back. Then the girls covered him with a towel from the waist down to his toes. Now, it looked like he was lying on his back with his legs straight. When someone would walk by, he would spring board up into a standing position, scaring them and causing most people to jump back. Soon, there were a lot of onlookers hanging out to watch him play his trick on unsuspecting people. After awhile, everyone just relaxed and soaked up the sun. When it was time to go, Abby looked up at her dad and thanked him for bringing the family to the beach. She said, "This is the best Spring break ever"!

Later that night, the girls were in their bedroom together when Abby asked Shelby if she knew that the Magic phone could make her disappear? Shelby said "No".

Abby then showed her that it has a cloaking feature and can make her disappear. Shelby said that was so cool and then told Abby that she needs to play a trick on Chad. "Oh yeah", what should I do", replied Abby? Shelby began whispering into Abby's ear so no one could hear, and they came up with a plan. Later, they filled in mom and dad on the joke. About an hour later, mom called everyone to dinner, and when Chad came to the table, you could tell that he got a little too much sun at the beach, from his red skin. You could also tell that he took a nap, because his hair was disheveled and his eyes were a little red. Basically, he was still out of it when he got to the table. Everyone began eating dinner and he didn't even realize Abby wasn't sitting next to him yet. Chad reached for the veggies and put them onto his plate; then, he scooped a spoonful of mashed potatoes and began to put them on his plate, but his plate moved over to the side just enough for him to miss the plate. The mashed potatoes ended up on the table, and Chad hadn't noticed yet. Then, he reached for a piece of grilled chicken and again, as he attempted to put it onto his plate, it moved on him causing the chicken to fall on the table, right into the mashed potatoes. Chad looked down and noticed most of his food was on the table. He let out and "Ah man" and said "what the heck just happened"?

It took a lot for everyone to keep a straight face, and dad asked him if everything was all right. He said, "yeah, but somehow I missed the plate". Just as he said that, the lights began to flicker. Still cloaked, Abby had gone over to the light switch and began moving the dimmer switch back and fourth, causing the lights to flicker in intensity. Everyone looked around at each other trying to figure out what was going on. It looked a little eerie as the lights were flickering. The lights then dimmed down so that it was much darker in the room and then a piece of chicken levitated off of a dish, and went into Abby's plate, which was right next to Chad.

Then, the vegetables and mashed potatoes followed, right into the plate. The next thing Chad saw was the fork lifting up off the table and scooping some mashed potatoes, as if a ghost were eating. Chad's eyes grew wide and he began to look like he was trying to yell, but he couldn't get any words out. Then a knife began to levitate up in the air and was waving around. Chad let out the loudest scream and took off for his room. He was officially freaking out! Everyone began laughing out so loud. That's when Abby reappeared, and you could see that she was laughing just as loud. Dad got up and turned up the lights, while mom went into Chad's room to get him. When he came back into the kitchen, everyone chuckled and he smugly laughed back, stating, "Yeah, real funny". The family got a kick out of Abby's new found antics, while learning her new found powers with her Magic phone.

Later that night, the kids decided to camp out in the living room. They set up a tent along with an inflatable mattress, and Abby brought her flashlight for a more realistic camping experience, and for increased theatrics while telling ghost stories! While the kids were in their tent, they began to talk about the stuff they wanted to do for the rest of their Spring break. Shelby asked Abby if she could take the family to Paris. She said that she's wanted to go to move to Paris. Chad said that he wanted to go back to Myrtle Beach, he thought their vacation there two summers ago was awesome. Abby said that she would love to do that and said "we should talk to mom and dad in the morning". Abby then said that she would like to go up to grammy and grandpas house, stating "we haven't seen them in awhile". Chad said, "When we go up to see grammy, we should stay for at least three days". So, he told the girls that we could put off Myrtle Beach for later, during summer break. They all agreed and would talk to mom and dad in the morning. They had a few snacks and eventually fell off to sleep.

The next morning, the kids talked about their plans with mom and dad and after a short debate, they all agreed to spend a few days in Paris and three days at grammy and grandpa's house. Abby called Pete and asked him a few technical questions about teleporting and how many people could go at once. He told her that, everyone in the family can go at the same time, but you will all have to hold onto each other very tight. While on the phone with Pete, mom interrupted Abby and asked if she could talk with him. Mom got on the phone and asked him that we can't just appear in Bethel at my mom and dad's house without a car. She said that she's not sure how to go about this! Pete reassured her and gave her a plan that would work out fine for their trip to Maine. Susan thanked Pete and asked him to wish us luck! He told her that everyone would be fine. She also asked Pete if he and Tillie wouldn't mind watching buttercup for the next two days. Pete said that would be fine.

Susan asked Abigail to hold onto Buttercup and take her over to Pete's house, that he was going to watch the dog for us, while in Paris. Abby tapped on Pete's address, picked up Buttercup, and within a "whoosh", delivered Buttercup to Pete and Tillie. While Abigail was taking care of the dog, dad made reservations for two nights in Paris and mom called grammy and grandpa to let them know that we were coming up to visit in three days. She said that we would be up there from Wednesday to Sunday. Susan then got on the phone to tell her brother and sister in law if they could make it to mom and dads' house for part of Spring break. They said that they would ask at work and if they could, they would make the trip. When mom told the kids that uncle Bill and aunt Edna would probably be coming, they all screamed out in excitement. They loved playing games and hanging out with them. Once everyone was ready and had their bags and backpacks packed, they met back in the living room. They all interlaced their arms together and Abby prepared the phone for travel. Once the information on Paris was entered into the Planet Earth app, she tapped go and with a whoosh, the family was gone. Within seconds, they all appeared on a sidewalk adjacent to avenue d'lena, right by the hotel with smiles on their face, because they were in Paris within the blink of an eye.

Once they looked each other over to make sure nothing was out of place, they walked up to the hotel. Phillip checked them in and they headed up to their room on the 6th floor. When they walked into their room, they were awestruck by the view that they had of the city. Shelby ran to the window in awe and couldn't believe that they were in the city that she's wanted to visit for so long. Shelby had taken French for the past three years and was ready to test her abilities with the language. Once the family was settled in, Phillip suggested an itinerary for the trip. He said that we don't have to have everything all planned out, but we should have an idea of what we want to do.

Shelby said that she wanted to visit a museum and all the others said that they wanted to see the Eiffel Tower. Phillip suggested that the family go out and walk towards the Eiffel Tower and try to blend in with the folks here in Paris. It wasn't hard finding the tower, because it was so tall and easy to see for miles. Phillip found a business that gave bike tours of Paris. So, he asked if everyone would like to see Paris by bike, and everyone agreed that that was a great idea. The tour took the group past the Louvre, Notre Dame, the Eiffel Tower, the banks of the Seine, and a visit to a local ice cream shop. After the ride, Shelby asked if they could visit the Louvre while here in Paris, and her dad said that would be great to do tomorrow.

As day turned to night, the family decided it was time to eat and finished with dinner and a great view of the Eiffel Tower. The tower was so beautiful at night, all lit up. The light made the tower look like it was made out of gold, and the city lights were beautiful lit up in the distance past the tower. Abigail was getting tired; so on the way back to the hotel, her dad picked her up and carried her all the way to the room. While Phillip tucked Abigail into bed, everyone else settled in to get some sleep. Susan got a call from her brother and when she answered, he told her that he and the family would be driving to mom and dad's house on Tuesday and should be there by Wednesday afternoon.

Susan was excited about the news and told Bill that we look forward to seeing them real soon. He asked Susan what they were up to and she told him that they were visiting Paris. He started to laugh and said, “Paris France”? She told him, “yes, and it’s so beautiful here”. He asked her how they were able to travel to Paris and then to Maine by Wednesday. She told him, that they have it all planned out and not to worry, little brother, and then hung up.

The next day, the family got up and went out on the terrace for breakfast. Susan told everyone that Uncle Bill and aunt Edna would be at grammy's and grandpa's house on the same day that we will arrive. The kids yelled out a big Yay!!!! They were excited about the news. Once they settled back down, Abigail said, “while we are in Paris, we need to have a buttered croissant for breakfast". So, she grabbed a croissant for everyone and gave them butter so that it was complete. They ate well this morning with milk, orange juice, fruit, cereal, and of course, their buttered croissant. After breakfast, the family was off to the Louvre for their date with the Mona Lisa. From the outside of the Louvre, you could see the glass pyramid, which was designed as a main entrance to the building. The outside of the building was awe inspiring, with all of it's ornate details.

The inside was even more impressive from the ornate designs in the building to all of the museum pieces found within. Abigail recognized the Mona Lisa from far away and wanted to get as close as possible to see all of it's details. Shelby, just learning about the Mona Lisa in school, began discussing the painting to the family. She said that Leonardo Da Vinci painted the Mona Lisa, and it was a portrait of a woman named Lisa del Giocondo, who was married to a wealthy silk merchant name Francesco del Giocondo. It's been said that Leonardo was commissioned to paint this portrait of her for their new home and in celebration of their new baby boy. Shelby went on to say it was painted between 1503 and 1506 in Florence Italy. In Italian, the name of the painting is La Gioconda, which means Jacond (happy or jovial), and the French title of the Mona Lisa is La Jaconde. Phillip was impressed at what Shelby knew about this painting, and told her that he was proud of her.

The family also got to see the sculpture of Venus De Milo, Liberty leading the People, Virgin of the Rocks, Psyche Revived, and many more art pieces that were just so beautiful. This was like spending the day in the past. Abby learned a lot about the Louvre too. When the Louvre was built back in the twelfth century by Phillip Augustus, it was designed as a fortress, on the west side of Paris, on the bank of the river Seine, to protect Paris from invaders from the north. As Paris grew so did its fortresses.

By the end of the day, the family was exhausted, because they had spent seven hours at the museum. It was time to head back towards the Eiffel Tower where they were going to have dinner right next to it, and then head back to the hotel for some rest.

The next day, was just as beautiful as the days before. It was time for the family to head back home, but they wanted to do one more thing. They wanted to go up to the top of the Eiffel Tower and see what was described as an amazing view of Paris. They needed to do this kind of fast so that they could check out on time from the hotel. So, Abigail set the coordinates of the hotel room as a returning point and then put in the coordinates of the Eiffel Tower. Abby tapped the Go To tab and with a whoosh, the family teleported to the tower. Abby said that she would have liked to get us all to the top of the tower, but didn't know how. She said that she would have to be there at least once before to set the coordinates in the phone to return to that same point. Phillip chuckled and said, "Are you kidding me"? "You transported us to Paris and know to the Eiffel Tower, and you're sorry that you couldn't get us up to the top"? He told Abigail, "Honey, you are amazing and there is nothing to be sorry about"! Abby smiled and said thank you.

The family got the tickets to go to the top of the tower and took the elevator up. Like everyone had said before, the view was beautiful. They could see all of the rooftops of the houses, hotels, and buildings for miles.

They could see the river Seine and the large lawn "Champ de Mars", formerly used by the French military as drilling and marching grounds. Abigail took in a deep breath and closed her eyes for a few minutes. She was so thankful to have experienced such a beautiful place here on earth. As the family wrapped up their trip, they huddled close together in a corner of the tower and Abby transported everyone back to the hotel room. They grabbed their luggage and within a "whoosh", they were back home in their small house on Long Island.

The kids took off outside and began playing, mindless of all the running they had done in Paris, and showing no signs of fatigue. Phillip asked Abigail to call Pete, and if he's home, to go over and pick up Buttercup. She said “sure dad”. Susan and Phillip went into their bedroom and took a nap, because they were exhausted. They slept for a few hours to regain what energy they could for the trip to Maine. Later that night, Susan told everyone to begin packing for our trip to grammy and grandpa's house; “we will be leaving tomorrow at around noon”. Chad asked if we were driving or teleporting up to Maine? Susan told him that we would be taking the minivan. He rolled his eyes and said "that stinks, eight hours in the van with my sisters, that's torture"! Susan just smiled and let him believe that.

Everyone began packing for their next trip, excited to see grammy and grandpa, and to be able to play in the great out doors. The next day, Phillip and Chad loaded up the minivan and by noon, the family was ready to head up to Maine. Shelby asked why we were leaving so late? Usually, we leave early in the morning. Susan told her that by the time we arrive in Bethel, you would probably just be waking up from a nap. Shelby then commented that by leaving now, we won't get up there until eight tonight, and that's too late. She said, “we'll see grammy and within two hours, we will have to go to bed”. Susan smiled and told Shelby to hold that thought. As everyone climbed into the minivan, Susan asked everyone to listen up. Dad closed all of the doors and put on his seatbelt. Susan said that this trip wasn't going to take a long time, but that what we do here must not be brought up with anyone, including grammy and grandpa. Chad asked, "What do you mean"?

Susan told everyone that we were going to try something that Pete said would work; we are going to teleport us along with the minivan and Buttercup up to Bethel. Chad and Shelby looked at each other in disbelief. Abigail had the Magic phone out already with coordinates to down town Bethel, off the beaten path. Abigail told everyone to hold onto each other tight. Shelby, you hold onto Buttercup and mom and dad, you guys hold onto the door handles with your free hands. Abby tapped on the Go To tab, and with a whoosh they were traveling at near the speed of light up to Maine. When the family arrived, they all had their eyes closed. The minivan was hot to the touch and smoke was coming off of the paint and out from underneath it. The whole family yelled out in cheer that they made it in this minivan safely. They were laughing as dad started up the van and began heading up to grammy and grandpa's house.

As the family drove through Bethel, they noticed how everyone was looking at them, almost as if they had three heads. Phillip thought that was odd and asked Susan what they were looking at. Susan just shrugged her shoulders and was dumbfounded. When they arrived, five minutes later, grandpa came out to greet the family. He hugged all of the kids first and then Susan. He asked Phillip "what happened to your minivan"? Phillip looked over at his car and saw that it had blackish smoke like marks along the sides of it. Phillip looked confused and said he had no idea. I think it was from the dirty roads and rain that we had coming up. He gave dad a hug and they all went inside to see grammy. Grandpa looked back at the minivan and thought how weird those marks looked, and that it didn't look like dirt and road grime. It reminded him of his work at NASA and the times that he saw marks all over the space capsules after they reentered the atmosphere.

When the kids went into the house, they all ran to grammy and gave her a big hug. It had been a long time since they had seen her last. Grammy asked how the kids were. You know, the usual stuff, the kids replied, "What have you guys been doing? How's school? How ya doing in dance, baseball, wrestling? The family continued talking for most of the afternoon. Grammy said that dinner would be ready at six. Just then, the phone rang; grammy talked for a few minutes and then hung up the phone. She told everyone, that uncle Bill, Aunt Edna, and your cousin Sierra would be here in about a half hour. The kids were excited to hear the news. Abby told grammy and grandpa that she loves coming up to visit, because we all have so much fun playing card games, badminton, and volleyball out in the front yard, and going for hikes through the woods and up the hill.

Chad yelled out to the girls and told them to come with him. They ran outside to the barn and Chad grabbed a couple of burlap bags. He gave the girls a bag and told them to follow him. They all ran down the road to two big trees, one on each side of the road. The trees were huge, and their branches hung over the road, actually touching each other in a few places. Chad told the girls that every time we would come up, he would climb these trees and sit above the road. He showed the girls where to get started and showed them that it's quite easy to climb these trees. But first, Chad said, "we have to fill the bags with leaves". So, they all began filling the bags up with leaves. Once they were done, they began their climb up the trunks of the trees and onto the thick branches that crossed over the road.

Chad told the girls, once they were in place, "now we wait for Uncle Bill and Aunt Edna". When they drive down the road and just before they get under us, drop the leaves all over their car. The girls started laughing and said that was a great idea. They waited about five minutes and they could hear a car coming towards them. It was a bright red Ford Fusion. Chad said that this is their car and to get ready. Just before the car drove under the branches, the kids dropped all of their leaves, right on top of the windshield and roof of the car. The car swerved a bit and Bill hit the brakes; you could hear what sounded like a loud commotion from within the car.

Then, Bill and Edna got out of the car, only to see the three kids laughing harder than they ever had before. Bill and Edna told them that they were in big trouble and when they get down from that tree, they were all going to get a whoopin. Abby yelled down at Edna and said that she was going to open a can of whoop cream on her, when she gets down. Edna started laughing and helped the girls down, but gave them a little swat on their butts as they got to the bottom. Bill went over to where Chad was coming down, and grabbed him before he got to the bottom and began spinning him around. Chad got real dizzy and could barely walk when Bill put him down. The great part was that they were all laughing, a great start to their vacation.

Bill told them to get in the car, with Sierra, and they drove the rest of the way up to the house.

Later that night, Abby took out the Magic Phone and began to evaluate everyone with the Medic app. Aunt Edna thought that was a fun little app that allowed Abby to play doctor. So, she told Abby that she wanted to be first. Abby began the scan procedure, typing in Edna's name, and then tapping start. Abby did a scan over Edna's body and after about one minute, it displayed her height, weight, blood pressure, heart rate, respiration, and a systems review that said all was clear. She showed it to aunt Edna after the scan and said, that's a neat little app. Of course, Edna didn't really think that it was nothing more than a toy, except that it did seem very accurate for a toy? As Abby scanned everyone, she would give them the results of the test when she was done, and no one really paid attention to what she was doing anyway, because they thought it was just a fun game for her.

Next was grammy. She asked grammy if she could check her vitals and do a check up on her. Grammy said "sure Dr. Abby, go ahead, I need a check up anyway". Grammy asked her if she wanted to be a doctor when she grows up and Abby told her that she wants to be a doctor, a physical therapist, and the President of the United States. Grammy was impressed and told her, "Wow, you sure do have a lot of initiative!" Abigail put in grammy's name and began the scan. Soon, grammy's vitals came up which were within normal limits; however, the scan tool detected a tumor within her left breast. Grammy asked how she was doing, and if she was going to live. Abby felt confused and upset, but somehow kept her emotions in check long enough to tell her grammy that she was fine. The Magic phone instructed Abby to place the infrared beam over the left breast and to line the beam over the X on the display, and then to press the start button until the display time reached zero. Abby told grammy that she had to do a few more tests and that it wouldn't take very long. Grammy said, "sure darling, do what you have to do", while smiling and playing with her grand daughter.

Abby lined up the infrared beam to the X on the display and tapped the start button. The laser light came on subtly, but began to intensify, while the phone began to emit a pulsating tone. Looking through the viewer and keeping her focus, Abby kept the infrared light right on the X the whole time. After about three minutes, the timer reached zero. The magic app then asked for another full body scan. Abby told grammy that she was almost done. I just have to do one more scan. Grammy just smiled and said "no problem doc". Abby did the scan and all of the vitals were displayed along with a systems review that was clean.

The medic app then displayed a report that it had eliminated a cancerous tumor from the left breast and that all was now within normal limits and no disease was found. Grammy asked Abby if she was going to be ok? Abby smiled and said "grammy you will be just fine"! Later that night, when Abby was tucked into bed, Susan asked if everything was ok with grammy. Abby looked up at her mother and said that the Magic Phone found a cancerous tumor in her left breast. Susan became upset and she started to cry. Abigail reached out and held her mother's hand, and said, "it's alright mom". The Magic Phone performed a procedure using its laser to kill the cancer. Grammy didn't even know, she thought I was just playing doctor. Her mother stopped crying and looked at Abigail. What are you saying Abby? She told her mother that after it killed the cancer, it did another full body scan and said that all systems are now within normal limits. Susan dropped down to Abigail and gave her a big hug, crying at the same time. Abby told her mom that everything would be alright.

The next morning, everyone woke up to the smell of pancakes and bacon. Abby ran down the stairs to find Chad already up playing a game of Uno with grandpa. Abby made her way into the kitchen where grammy was making breakfast. Abby asked if she could help out and of course grammy said "sure, would you take care of making the scrambled eggs"? Abby agreed and began cracking the eggs. She put in a little milk, some salt and pepper and poured it into the hot pan. Grammy said that she was doing a great job, while Abby slowly stirred the eggs around in the pan. Grammy yelled up for everyone to come down for breakfast. The whole family gathered around the table and enjoyed a great breakfast prepared by grammy and Abigail.

Phillip said that he would like to hike up to the top of the mountain this morning for some fresh air and to get some exercise, and that we will have a great view of the town below. The girls said that they were going to go shopping except for Abby and Shelby, they wanted to go on a hike to the top of the mountain with dad and uncle Bill. When breakfast was done, they all washed the dishes and cleaned the kitchen. When everyone dispersed, Susan asked her mother "how's everything"? Her mother replied that she was doing well. She talked about the flowers and vegetables that she just planted in the garden, and how she's been helping at the church with their fundraisers.

Susan was trying to get an idea for how her mom was physically feeling; so, she asked "how have you been feeling, have you seen the doctor lately"? Her mom told her that she had been feeling great, but the oddest thing. Susan asked her, "What"? Her mother replied that she woke up this morning and felt a mild burning sensation, with a red mark on her left breast, and wondered if she should go check it out? Susan told her that it's never a bad idea to have it checked out, "an ounce of prevention is worth a pound of cure"!

It was time to climb the mountain! Phillip grabbed the Magic pack and threw it over his shoulders, just in case anyone got thirsty up on the hill. Abby was very enthusiastic at first, but after an hour she got really tired. Everyone reached the top after about an hour and a half, but you could hear Abby complaining about how tired and thirsty she was. Once at the top, there was a great panoramic view of the surrounding mountains and valleys. Phillip asked Abby if she could fill up the Magic Pack with water and some healthy snacks. Abby took out her phone, and at first glance, she noticed an update had occurred over night. She closed the update screen and opened up the food & water app to order all of the snacks. Phillip could feel the pack get heavy; so, he opened it up and handed out the waters and snacks to everyone, while they enjoyed the beautiful view. On the hike back down, the kids said that there was going to be a race to the house. Bill was all about the race; he had a long stride and could outrun everyone there. So, he took off down the hill.

Abby asked Shelby to hang out next to her, she had a plan. She opened up the planet earth app and located their position. She scrolled over to where the house was and held onto Shelby's hand, and tapped go. Within a second they were standing next to the house. They looked at each other and then ran over to the porch, where they laid back on the recliners as if nothing unusual had just happened. After about ten minutes, they could hear Uncle Bill coming down through the woods, yelling that he was in first place. The girls stood up at the edge of the porch and started laughing.

When Bill saw the two of them standing on the porch, all the excitement left his face. He was bewildered at how they got down to the house so fast. He asked Shelby how they did it? She said that we know a shortcut that is a secret. You could hear Bill saying under his breath "Ah man"! "Somehow you two cheated". About five minutes later, dad and Chad came down from the hill, and when they saw the two girls standing up on the porch, they knew exactly what happened. As they walked up on the porch, they told the girls that they were big fat cheaters! The girls smiled and began laughing. Shelby said that we didn't cheat; we know a secret shortcut, LOL.

Later, the girls asked dad if they could go into Bethel, and he said that was fine, but to be careful and to stay out of trouble. The two of them walked down the road a bit and once away from everyone's view, transported down to Bethel. They went into the shops and looked at the souvenirs, clothing, and jewelry. Shelby found a necklace that she liked that had a blue gem stone on it, and said that she would love to have something like that for her birthday or next Christmas. Abby said that it was beautiful. She showed Shelby a bracelet that she liked and found two necklaces that would be perfect for mom and grammy.

The two continued on their way, down the street, and reached a skate park. They watched a few kids riding their scooters and skateboards down the walls and through the two bowls. As they sat there and watched for a while, Abby went into her currency app and took out some money. She could only take out one hundred dollars a day. She tapped on the send money tab and it was sent to the Magic pocket in her pants. She decided that by the end of their vacation, she was going to surprise a few people.

Shelby told Abigail that they needed to go back home. So, they started back and when they reached a restaurant, they asked the waiter if they could use the bathroom. He told them “no problem” and pointed them to where the bathrooms were. Once they were alone, in the bathroom, they teleported back up to grammy's house. After about five minutes, the waiter asked one of the waitresses to go into the bathroom and look for the two girls, because he hadn't seen them come out and was worried. The waitress came back out and said there weren't any girls in the bathroom! The waiter looked dumbfounded, he knew that he saw them go in but he didn't see them come out.

The next day, Abigail looked at the upgrade that was downloaded. She had never seen an upgrade before. So, she went to settings, upgrades, and then clicked on the upgrade to read about it's contents. The instructions described that the Magic phone will stay in continuous communication with the user, through the ear piece or the built in microphone, and that you can communicate and request commands just by speaking to it. It referred to section 15.0 in the MDF for full instructions on this update.

Abigail read the update within the MDF and was ready to use this new feature. She walked outside and saw mom and grandpa throwing the Frisbee. She said open camera and the camera app opened. She asked if they would pose for a picture and of course, that wasn't a problem. So, they came together for a photo. Abby aimed the camera and said, "take picture", and the camera took the shot. Abby told them “thank you”. She walked away and her mom and grandpa continued on with their game of Frisbee. When Susan threw the frisbee, Abigail said push pointing the phone towards the Frisbee as it was flying through the air, and pushed the Magic Phone forward causing the Frisbee to blow about 50 feet off course. Grampy told Susan, “Great throw” and laughed at her.

Abigail then walked into the woods, looking around for the biggest oak tree she could find. When she found one, she commanded, "laser medium" and while aiming along the top edge of the phone, she fired the laser with the thumb button. Abigail could see how the laser was burning into the wood and after about 10 seconds she stopped firing. She then commanded the laser to high-intensity and fired at the tree, and within five seconds she had cut the tree in half, causing it to fall to the ground, with the trunk and stump still on fire as the tree lied on the ground. The leaves next to the tree began to catch on fire, Abigail hesitated for a few seconds, and then commanded freeze. She pushed the trigger and froze the base of the tree, and the area next to it, causing the fire to go out.

Abby began to sense a feeling, as if she was becoming one with the Magic Phone, an anthropomorphization if you will. The commands and actions were becoming more reflexive to her, a sense that she was beginning to really understand the capabilities of the phone, a lot better. As Abby stepped out of the woods and onto the road, she decided to Cloak herself, but she thought about changing her identity for some fun. Abby opened up the cloaking app and tapped on the identity tab. She selected female and Native American as the nationality, and then began looking through all of the photos. She selected a photo of a beautiful Indian girl and then tapped the cloak tab. Abigail didn't feel any different after she was cloaked; so, she thought to turn on her camera and reversed the view. She was able to look at herself through the camera, and to her surprise, she looked amazingly different.

She put her phone away and started walking by grammy and grandpa's house. She could see that everyone was still outside playing in the front yard and began to feel a little nervous that someone would be able to see through her disguise, but on the contrary, everyone stopped what they were doing to watch this young Native American princess walk by. Abby waived to everyone and continued walking down the street. When Chad saw this girl, he thought it was love at first sight! Little did he know that it was really Abigail. Once she was in the clear, she tapped on the stop tab and instantly changed back to herself. Just as she got back up to the yard, everyone had gathered around to play hide and seek.

Abby asked if she could play and everyone said sure. Aunt Edna told everyone that the base would be the front porch, and that you can't hide beyond the woods, you would have to stay within the yard and barn area. Everyone agreed and then picked straws to see who would be the seeker first, and uncle Bill picked the shortest straw, so he was “it”. Aunt Edna said that he would have to count to twenty and then shout out "ready or not, here I come".

Everyone took off to hide, and Abby thought to herself, that she's going to make this game very interesting. On the first go, she cloaked herself, becoming invisible to everyone. When uncle Bill walked right by her to find someone, she walked up to the porch and turned off the cloaking. When uncle Bill was over by the barn, she yelled out to him "uncle BIll, I'm over here"!!! He looked up and couldn't believe that he had somehow missed her. Just then, he heard a faint clank in the garbage can, and snuck up on it, and with a swift movement, pulled the garbage can lid off and tagged Chad. Everyone started laughing and met back at home base. Grammy and grandpa said that this was fun and that they haven't had this much excitement and fun in such a long time.

Now, it was Chad's turn to be it. He began counting to twenty slowly and everyone took off again. Grammy and grandpa hid in the truck by the barn, Phillip went up into a tree along the properties edge and he helped Susan up as well. They had a great view of the entire yard from there. Shelby hid behind the tractor, and Edna and Bill hid behind the big boulders that lined the back edge of the property. Abigail on the other hand, slid the speed dial all the way to the right of the slide rule, max speed, and turned it on.

When she started walking back around the house, she saw some unusual things. Chad was just turning around on the porch, but looked frozen. She could tell that he was in the middle of saying something by the position of his mouth and lips. Abby began to walk around the yard and could see where everyone was hiding. She found all of her family in their hiding places, but no one was moving. When she walked back over to Chad, he was now on the steps, heading into the yard. She pushed him forward causing him to fly off of the steps, but in slow motion to her. From everyone else's perspective, he flew off the last two steps very fast and onto the ground.

Abigail ran down to town and saw cars on the road with people in them but moving at a very slow pace. She walked right in front of a semi-truck that was on the highway without hesitation, because she was moving so fast. Abigail was heading into the jewelry store to get the jewelry she picked out for her sister, mom, and grammy. Once in the store, she saw three people moving very slowly, that you couldn't detect movement unless you stayed in one place for about five minutes. Abigail began to take the jewelry out of the window case, when she remembered hearing things from the past. She began to recall her mom and dad telling the kids not to ever steal something from anyone, "that is stealing, and you wouldn't want anyone to do that to you"! She also remembered her lessons at church, ten weeks going over the Ten Commandments, and she remembered the eighth commandment "Thou Shalt Not Steal". Abby had paused for a minute while pondering her actions, and one of the workers, who happened to look down at the cabinet door briefly, saw her for a split second. In real time the sales woman thought she saw a girl down on her knees looking up at her, but then she was gone. Hmm, it must have been my imagination the sales woman thought.

In no time at all, Abigail had made it back up the hill to the house. She stood up on the porch and looked out at Chad who was running around the rocks to get uncle Bill. To Abby, they still looked frozen in time. She pulled out the Magic phone and shut off the speed dial, and all of a sudden Chad was running in real time again, running after Uncle Bill, while Edna was running the other way and up towards the porch.

Susan and Phillip were coming down from the tree and ran to the porch, SAFE they shouted! You then saw Shelby peaking out from around the tractor and then running to base. Chad was able to catch uncle Bill before he made it to base, and now he was it. Grandpa and grammy made their way out of the truck slowly, but successfully hiding from Chad. The games continued throughout the afternoon and everyone had a great time. Susan and grammy made a great dinner for everyone, and while at the table, they all talked about how much fun they had. Tomorrow would be the last day of their spring break, and everyone would be going home.

The next morning, Abby opened up the currency app and requested another one hundred dollars. She took the money out of her pocket and by this day, she had collected three hundred dollars in total. After breakfast, she asked mom if they could drive downtown, that she wanted to get a gift for Shelby and grammy. Susan thought that would be a great idea, and they drove down the hill to Bethel. Abigail was excited and wanted to surprise everyone, and when she entered the store, she knew exactly what to pick out.

She had enough money to also buy aunt Edna a beautiful bracelet. Abby asked her mom if she could step outside for a moment, that she had a little surprise for her too. The sales lady told the little girl that she looks very familiar, and feels that she's seen her somewhere before, or maybe it was in a dream. Abby remembers the woman; she was the same person standing behind the counter the day before. The woman was very nice and wrapped the jewelry for Abigail, so that she could give the gifts to everyone when she got home.

While the family sat down for their last lunch together, Abigail took out her presents and gave them to the ladies. Aunt Edna was very surprised that a young girl, in these days and times, would think of others the way that she does. Each of the girls gave Abby a great big hug and thanked her for their gifts. Grammy asked Abigail to come over to her and told her that she is very proud of her and loves her very much. Abby smiled and gave grammy a great big hug again, telling her "I Love you very much too"! Before you knew it, it was time to leave and head home. Uncle Bill and aunt Edna decided to stay an extra day, so they were able to waive off the family too. Everyone got into the minivan and started down the driveway. The three kids put their windows down and yelled out, as they were driving down the road, "Bye, we'll see you later, Love you, miss you, see you later"!!!

Once they had driven south of Bethel, Phillip holding onto the steering wheel with his left hand and his right hand was holding Susan's hand. The rest of the family held onto each other and Shelby held onto Buttercup; as they were driving, Abigail teleported the whole family and minivan right back to Bellport New York. Abigail had located a destination on Sunrise highway and you should have seen the tires when the minivan made contact with the pavement! Some smoke came off the tires initially, and then they caught up to speed. The minivan was now about fifty feet in front of a few other cars that were already on the highway. Abby looked out the windows to see how close they were to traffic, and could see that the people behind them were unsure of what just happened. Abigail told her dad, that the people behind us look a little surprised that we are in front of them.

The spring break was an awesome time for everyone, but especially for Abby. She had learned a lot about the Magic phone and how to use it, becoming more intuitive with this amazing device. School was now in session and the kids were back to their normal routines.

Chapter Thirteen

Meeting of the Minds

The weather began to warm, the grass was green and plush, and the flowers were now all blooming on Long Island. It was the first week of June, on a relaxing Saturday. Abigail and Shelby were out riding their bikes and Chad was inside watching a Yankees game. Phillip was excited about the nice weather, because he was able to get out and prepare the Shelby GT500KR for a car show. In addition, he had recently finished his 289 FIA Cobra for race day, and would be taking it to several road course tracks this summer. Susan was out back in her garden tending to her flowers and soaking up the sun.

When Shelby and Abigail were done with their bike ride, they ran inside to see what Chad was doing. They asked him to go outside with them so that they could ride their bikes together, down by the sump. He said that he may go out later, but wanted to watch the game. Shelby asked him how much longer before the game is over? He said that the game just started and was still in the first inning. Shelby and Abby were looking at each other, and you could tell that Abby had an idea. Shelby asked her what she was thinking about? "Well, I was thinking that we go to the game"! Why watch it here in the living room, when we can watch it right there at the stadium. After all, we haven't been to a game in so long, and we'll get to see it first hand.

Chad sat up to attention and looked over at Abby, and shouted "Yeah, that's a great idea"! Abby began to study the television, and she noticed something. Abby told the other two to watch, and she explained that every time the camera was on the batter, you could see the rows of seats, and which seats were filled and which were empty. She asked them to look three rows up, in the middle, stating, “They are empty”. Abigail took the Magic phone out and opened up the map application. She zoomed into where the stadium was located, right down to the section, and placed her marker as close as she could to the three empty seats. The Go To tab became active on the phone, and she said that she was ready.

Chad ran into his room to put a Yankees hat on along with his jersey. Abby asked everyone to sit down on the couch and said that she needed to time this departure just right, because there were so many people around their destination. She quietly told the two to hold hands and she took Shelby's left hand with her right. Abby watched the pitch and sure enough, the batter hit a ball so hard that it went high up into the outfield stands. She hit the Go To tab, and with a whoosh, they were no longer in the house.

Within a few seconds, they went from sitting on the couch to sitting in three chairs at the stadium. Everyone in the stadium was standing and cheering, the kids looked at each other with smiles on their faces, but at the same time a little bit of a worried look too, because they didn't want anyone to see them transport like this. Abigail was pretty close with the location of the seats, almost perfect; her and Shelby were in empty seats, but Chad, just then, was sat on by one of the fans who had been standing for the home run. After the man sat down on Chad's lap, he jumped up, turned around and said "hey, whatsamattaforyou"! "Get out of my seat kid".

Chad apologized and the kids moved down one seat. The three of them were giggling about Chad getting sat on and scolded by this man. Chad said that it wasn't funny! The girls just burst out laughing! Nevertheless, they all began to watch and exciting baseball game as Abby admired the huge stadium and all the people in it. After a few innings, Abby noticed a faint voice that was slowly getting louder; she turned around and could hear a man saying, "hot dogs, get your hot dogs". She got excited and asked if anyone wanted a hot dog? Shelby said that she would like one and Chad asked for two. Abby called the man over and bought five dogs, giving the first one to the man sitting next to Chad. She said that we would like to buy you a hot dog for scaring you like that earlier. He said that she didn't have to do that, but Abby insisted. The man said thank you and told the kids that they were alright.

At home, Susan and Phillip came in the house to have lunch. Susan prepared a few sandwiches while Phillip poured the milk. They both sat down on the couch and began to watch the game that was still on television. All of a sudden Susan shouted out, "Oh my Gosh, oh my gosh, where are the kids"? Phillip said that he didn't know. Susan told him that she knew where they were, and he replied where? Look there, pointing over to the TV. "When they show the batter at home plate again, look into the seats, up about three rows". The two of them looked closely at the TV and sure enough, they could see their kids at the stadium.

Phillip called Abigail on her phone and asked her what she and the other two were doing? First, she hit the other kids to get their attention and whispered “its dad”! She told dad that they were out playing. He said, "oh really, that's funny”. “What's all of that noise"? Abby replied that it was nothing. It almost sounds like you're in a stadium full of baseball fans, exclaimed Phillip. He told her that mom and I can see all three of you right now, and it doesn't look like you guys are outside playing. Abby began to look around for her father, but couldn't see him. She asked him, "where are you? I don't see you". He said, "I see you on the TV"! “What are you doing at the Yankees game”, and why wouldn't you invite mom and I"? He told her after the game to come straight home. She agreed and told the other two that they were busted, that mom and dad can see us on TV. Abby told them to look over at that camera before the next pitch and wave to mom and dad.

It wasn't long before the game ended and the kids were back in the house, bragging about how much fun the game was and that Chad was lucky enough to have several team players autograph his hat.

The night before, Abigail called Pete to see what he was doing on Sunday, and She’s wanted to see him for quite some time. They made plans, in the afternoon to get together, so that she could learn more about the Magic phone, and learn more about the people from Gmack. Abby asked her dad if it was ok to visit with Pete and Tillie and he said “certainly, but it will have to be after church”. She let her dad know that she scheduled the visit for the afternoon so that she wouldn't miss church. “After all, I enjoy going to church, seeing all of my friends, and wouldn't want to miss it". Abby's dad said it would be fine then.

The morning went by so fast, and before she knew it, it was time to make a visit to see Pete and Tillie. Abby had some tough questions for Pete to answer today! She told everyone goodbye and whooshed off to Pete's house. She got her hugs from Tillie and headed down into the laboratory. Pete was sitting next to his workstation and turned around as Abby made her way down the stairs. He gave her a hug and asked her if she would like something to drink. She said no thanks, that she had a few drinks in her magic pack already. "So, I hear you have some questions for me", exclaimed Pete. Abby said that she would like to know as much about the phone as possible and I want to hear more about the people from Gmack.

Abby asked him for guidance into the right schools too, so that she can learn as much as he knows. Pete laughed and told her that she is very smart and that he would help her with finding a great school. Pete reached into a drawer under the bench and pulled out two cases. He told Abigail that he would like her to have this. She opened a case to reveal a real cool pair of glasses. Pete told her that the Magic phone was, for the most part, completed about twenty-five years ago, and I finished these glasses a few years later. Pete demonstrated the glasses for Abby with his pair. He showed her the lenses and how they could go from clear to darker depending on how much ambient light there was. He said that there is a microphone and earpiece on the right blade of the glasses, which allows you to communicate with the phone. Oh, and this can be turned off if you have your earring in.

At night, you can turn on the glasses, which will give you night vision capabilities, with Infrared assist, so you can see in the darkest of dark situations, and a soft glow on the backside of the glasses is normal in the dark.

Pete then asked Abby to put her glasses on. "Now, we have to pair the glasses to your phone". "Go into settings and click on the connect tab". “Once you're there, tap the SFD tab, that is spectacle forward display". "Move the slider to the on position and the phone is paired with the glasses". "Wha Lah, it's that easy"! Now, watch all of the displays start up while wearing your glasses. You can see everything from your phone while wearing these, including maps, the Gateway browser, the weather, what ever you want, even texting via voice command! Abby thought that this was so cool.

Pete showed her the on, off, and auto button on the right blade of the glasses. In auto, the lenses will change from normal lenses to night vision based on the incoming ambient light. Pete switched her glasses to auto and put them on her face. Pete said, "Great fit, now let me turn off the lights down here". When the lights went out, it got very dark for a few seconds, and then the glasses night vision activated and she could see pretty good at first. She noticed that the glasses started off rather dim and the light increased over time. Abigail asked Pete if that was normal? He told her that you wouldn't want to walk out of a dark house into a lot of sunlight very fast, because you wouldn't be able to see for awhile. So, I made these glasses to intensify slowly, so that it doesn't blind you. "Understood" Abby replied.

Abby got up and walked around the dark laboratory, getting used to the glasses. She could see Pete looking around with his glasses on, as if he were a kid trying out a new toy. He turned towards Abby and said, "I still think these are the coolest glasses I've ever seen, if I do say so myself". Abby laughed and told him that he's a very smart man, and a perfectionist and it shows in your work. She asked Pete a question, "do you know what I like most about you"? Pete replied, "Well, I don't know, my good looks"? Abigail laughed again and she said, "no, besides your good looks, I like that you are such a caring man and you have shown me nothing but love and kindness". Pete just smiled and told her thank you. Pete then turned the lights back on and the glasses automatically tuned off of the night vision mode.

Pete told Abigail that she will become more fluent with the use of the phone over time and with practice. He suggested that she get into the simulator, because that will teach her how to use the Magic phone more proficiently. Pete told her, "If you want to be a professional, you have to constantly practice and the simulator app will allow to do that. He told her that when she learned how to fly on the beach, that maybe she should have done that in the simulator, because it would have been much safer. Abby promised to use the simulator for training from now on.

Pete asked Abby, "What else did you want to talk about"? She said that she would like to learn more about the people from Gmack. Pete began to tell her a story of his time with the aliens and much of what he had learned. Pete told Abby that during the three months that I spent with Anshar and Kishar, I learned so much about their values, society, government, education, eating habits, rituals, and the technology that they possessed". First, Anshar was a male and Kishar was a female. They were in love and cared for each other immensely, and the government of Gmack preferred that two mates travel together because they would be with each other throughout their lives". The two of them told me that both of our worlds are in a dimension separate from our creator, and that we will never be able to cross that dimensional plane until we die. Anshar told me that our soul, which is pure energy, will cross the plane, but our flesh will not. Kishar said "we believe that the master of this dimension will call us back home when we die". Anshar also told me "one thing that we do know on Gmack, is that we we're not formed from a lightning strike into a puddle of water, creating a single celled organism, which eventually leads to the evolution of us". "We were created with purpose, just like all of the man made objects all around us".

Man creates things for a purpose, not by chance. Anshar said that there are common elements in the universe, which are the building blocks of life, but you need a designer and an engineer to put all of those individual elements together and into motion. Pete said, "simply put, a cake just doesn't happen". "Abby, you have to put the ingredients together precisely, and bake it for a specific time, for it to be good". "Also, this Magic phone didn't just appear on the beach one day, and then I found it". "No, I created this phone, which has multiple systems, consisting of thousands of components". "Just like our bodies"! Oh and when it comes to which came first, the chicken or the egg, it's always been the chicken".

Pete continued to tell Abigail that Anshar and Kishar looked just like us, but their eyes are about 5mm larger than ours. They have pure white hair, and their brains are the same size; but, more area of the brain is used for processing and storing information, along with the neurons used for transmitting information from one area of the brain to the other, like ours. They mate just like we do, and their language is closest to resembling the Sumerian and Akkadian languages, and they have picked up on all of our languages over the centuries. In fact, Anshar and Kinshar could speak twenty-five languages from earth. Abby told

Pete, "that's amazing, I can barely speak a second language".

Abby asked Pete to go on! Pete said that they have been watching us, here on earth, for approximately seven thousand years, and began helping humans for the past five thousand years. The help was sporadic and kept very secret. Not everyone was privy to this information, only leaders of tribes and countries. Over the past thousand years, they have backed off on assisting us and our technology. They mainly just observe us now. Abby asked, "who did they help out the most"? He said that they helped out the Egyptians and the Roman Empire, giving them vast amounts of technological know how. At one point, several of the people from Gmack procreated with humans here on earth, and at that point stayed here on earth until they past away. The children of these couples would go on to become Kings and Queens, and lead their nations, but in the end, evil would eventually come to rule and wipe out all of what they created over centuries of time, losing much that they had gained in technology for future generations to experience and to improve upon. Pete explained that Anshar told me, that humans lost a thousand years of technological advances in the Middle Ages alone, and that technology is destroyed from people who start wars and try to obliterate all that other people have. Pete said that wars must stop, and the people of Gmack do not condone war. They have fought to keep their people safe, and despise war. “Which brings up a point”, Pete exclaimed, "we have to keep our technology a secret at all times. It's government that takes technology and turns it into tools of war, and this will never happen with the Magic phone.

"In the near future, I will ask you to keep tabs on me as I have kept tabs on you, and if either of us get into trouble or cornered to give up this technology, the other person will help out the other to prevent that from happening. Abby, you will become my security, as I have been your security over the past year".

"Nevertheless, where was I"? "Oh yeah, both Anshar and Kishar took in all of my data and scientific work that I've been working on for decades and documented it". For the most part, they said that it was quite primitive, but showed them that we as humans have made a lot of progress over the past three hundred years. They were able to answer all of my questions to help me figure out what I was not able to answer myself, or my scientific colleagues. Then, they started to share technology that provided me with ninety percent of what makes this phone work. Abby asked, "what happened to them after they died"? Pete told Abigail that the government ordered autopsies on the bodies and the autopsies started at the lab here at Brookhaven.

Rumors began to increase about the aliens being here on site; so, the government decided to move them to a secret facility out in Nevada. There, they continued with the autopsies and later preserved the bodies in cryo chambers. They have also dismantled the ship that they flew in, and have used the technology over the past fifty years in aeronautics and electrical engineering. The only thing that they never got a hold of were the communicators. I understood how they worked, electronically, and kept them from the government. "Abby, the communicators were way more advanced then the space ship that they flew in". When they were to return to Gmack, they were going to teleport back rather than fly back in their ship. The technology in the Magic phone was created during their space flight to earth. So, Gmack uploaded the schematics, on how to build them, to their onboard flight computers.

We began the project together, right here on Long Island, and we worked on the project for about two months before they died. Pete said that he wasn't able to transport them home in time, because the government took the bodies before I was finished with the Magic phone. Pete said, "I've always wanted to get to them, so that I could send their bodies back home to Gmack". Abby told Pete that we can do that together. All we need are coordinates of where Anshar and Kinshar's bodies are kept and a plan to transport them back to Gmack. Pete told Abigail that security is the issue on whether we can complete the task or not. He said that they are somewhere between three and four stories underground and the areas are locked down by bomb blast doors that are made out of steel, that is three feet thick, and weigh thirty tons each. These doors are only opened once a week to let in an oncoming crew and to let out the crew that has worked there for the past week.

On top of that, the door is only open for five minutes. Abby said that is cake work, no problem. "Let's do this for Anshar and Kinshar and all the people of Gmack". Pete, took in a deep breath and exhaled, looked at Abby, and said "alright, I will do it with you"!

Chapter Fourteen

Infiltrating Area 51

Pete and Abigail planned the mission to the infamous Area 51, for about a month. Abby had heard a lot of rumors, but was about to see this area first hand. She trusted Pete with his knowledge of the area and his expertise, and looked forward to this mission with him. She knew that it was for a good cause and it would let the people of Gmack know that their people are cared for by another race, who in the end, are really just like them. Abigail was always trying to do the right thing, by helping people, every since she was a little girl, and this situation was no different.

During the past month, they visited the area on several occasions, mapping out the exact location of the buildings, the activity within those buildings, and security schedules. To accomplish this task without getting caught was not as difficult as Pete first thought. The two teleported to a small area outside of the base, and once there, they would open up the speed dial application and slide the tab all the way to the right, for max speed. At that point, all they had to do was keep moving to prevent from being seen.

On a Thursday, they watched a plane arrive, which was delivering the new crew that would start their shift for the next week. The crew entered the south hanger that faces the flight line, and from there, they would descend a staircase, walk through a tunnel, and ascend another staircase to the north hanger that faces the flight line. From this point, the new crew would muster in the middle of the hanger. Once everyone was accounted for and the pass down was given, the exiting crew left the same way the first crew came in. Once the old crew exited the building, the hanger floor began to descend, moving the workers, who were still in formation, underground. Pete noted that once the hanger floor returned to its normal position, the thirty-ton bomb blast door would open, the crew would walk through the doorway and then the door would close. As far as Pete knew, this door and the hanger floor elevator would stay locked for a full week, unless they would move an aircraft from the build facility up to the hanger.

The two teleported back home and were to meet for a final briefing next Wednesday to go over the final plan and procedures to teleport Anshar and Kinshar home. During that week, Abigail decided to practice moving around at full speed on the speed dial. She had security cameras at her house and wanted to see if they would detect her if she stopped moving at different time intervals. She started out by walking at a normal pace, and then stood still for exactly one minute. Afterwards, she ran over to the computer and replayed what the cameras picked up. What she saw on the screen was very interesting. She could see that when she was walking and for up to thirty seconds of standing still, she couldn't be seen at all; but, after thirty seconds, she could faintly see and aberration of her body, and as the time reached a full minute, she could see herself quite well. Once she started walking again after standing still for a minute, she disappeared again. So, she knew that her and Pete would need to keep moving at all times, or only pause for twenty five seconds or less to remain undetected. She called Pete and told him of her little experiment. He agreed with her conclusion and said that he would adopt her new measure to stay concealed, once they are onsite at Area 51.

It wasn't long before Wednesday came, and the two met at Pete's house. Tillie told them that they couldn't leave until they both ate a good breakfast. Pete told her that he didn't need to eat and would be just fine, but Tillie would have nothing to do with that and began making breakfast. Abby agreed with Tillie and said, “Just listen to her and be happy”. Pete said "yes dear" and went about his planning with Abby. Pete went over all the details with Abby from start to finish and then had breakfast. Tillie made them some fruit to start off their breakfast and then gave them scrambled eggs, a slice of bacon, toast and a glass of orange juice. When they were done with breakfast, Tillie told them that they could go now. They gave her a hug and told her that they would be back by the end of the day.

Pete confirmed the coordinates for the trip in his phone and made sure Abby’s were the same. On a count of three, they tapped the Go To tabs and the same time and with a whoosh, they were gone. Within seconds, they were standing in a remote location of Area 51. They both immediately went to speed dial and moved the slider all the way to the right and tapped the start tab. They began their walk down a long stretch of road to the hanger facility and assessed the area. They could see security personnel patrolling by foot and trucks. Abby thought this was the coolest mission that you could ever go on, because she could walk right up to a security officer who was moving at a normal pace in real time, but was standing still compared to the speed that her and Pete were traveling at. She began to play with the security detail a little bit, while they waited for the plane to arrive. She quickly moved from one guard to the other turning their hats around so they were facing backwards. When a supervisor came by, he yelled at all of them for being unprofessional. They looked at each other with bewilderment and then turned their hats back around. Pete rolled his eyes when he saw what she was doing next and then started to laugh. Abby went over to one of the guards who just happened to be standing next to another guard. She bent down and tied his shoelaces together and then walked back over to Pete who was walking around the area to keep from being detected. He told her that she shouldn't be having so much fun. Just then, they could hear the guard yelling out in slow motion as he slowly began to fall forward onto the ground. After the guard fell, he began to yell at the other guard, thinking that he had tied his shoelaces together as a prank. The other guard had no idea how it happened and said that he didn't do it. A few of the other guards saw what was happening and started laughing out loud. Everyone was laughing including Pete and Abby, while the guard was untying the knot in his laces.

Abby just thought of an idea and told Pete to hang on and watch. She quickly went by each of the guards and took their two-way radios and placed them in front of the front tire to a moving truck and by the time anyone knew that their radio was gone, the truck had run them all over. Abby started laughing and Pete just smirked. He told her that she needs to be a good girl now and stay focused on the mission. While the guards were standing around trying to fix their radios, Pete could see the plane touching down on the runway. He told Abby that it was time to move into action. When the crew egressed the aircraft, Pete and Abby

began their walk into the hanger and made their way through the tunnel to the north hanger that faced the flight line. Once in the hanger, they could see the middle section of the hanger floor begin to descend. Pete never thought about this part of the crews procedure.

The deck had to lower to pick up the outgoing crew from the underground facility! Pete yelled to Abby and told her to jump down onto the descending hanger deck and then jump to the floor before it reaches the bottom. As they were descending together, which seemed very slow compared to the speed they're traveling at, Pete could see that the blast door was still open. He told Abby to follow him and they ran through the doorway and began to look all over for the two aliens from Gmack. They went past several aircraft including helicopters that he had never seen before. As they worked their way further back, Pete began to see aircraft that looked more and more like the space craft that landed fifty-five years ago at Brookhaven lab. Pete saw a sign that said "R&D1" on it, and took that to mean research and development one, the original ship.

Pete asked Abby to follow him down a short but wide corridor that opened up into a large room, and in the center of this room was the original spacecraft. Half of it was intact and the other half was dismantled into small parts, as if people had dissected it apart to see how it worked and what it was made out of. There were computers all over the place with design programs running, drawing boards with phases of planning and prototype designs shown. As Pete and Abby walked around the spacecraft, they saw two glass enclosures and within those glass cases were the two bodies of Anshar and Kinshar. Abby's eyes were wide open, she stood silent until Pete told her to keep moving around the cases so that we're not seen. She asked

Pete, "are these the two aliens that you worked with a long time ago"? Pete told her that this is Anshar and Kinshar. “We have to teleport them to Gmack now and get out of here before the next crew makes there way down, and the doors close”. “Once both of those doors close, I don't believe we can teleport, without enough signal from the atmosphere and space”. “I’ve also developed an app that will allow me to lock onto an object and transport that object without me accompanying it”. Pete had his Magic phone out and opened up the teleport app. He locked on the two glass pods through the front screen on the phone. He plugged in a location on Gmack and tapped the Go tab. Within a second, the two pods with the alien's bodies were gone.

"Now, let's get out of here Abby", shouted Pete. They began their way back through the hallways to get out. Pete took a few photos of the projects on the drawing boards, while he was exiting the underground facility. He thought that he could look at these later to see what the crew is working on. Abby yelled to Pete, that the crew just started coming through the bomb blast door and she could see the hanger floor elevator heading back up. The two of them weaved through the men who were walking forward, but at the same time it looked like they were standing still. Pete accidentally bumped one of the guys, knocking him to the ground. From the crewman’s perspective, he had no idea what hit him as he flew down to the ground. A few of his co-workers helped him back up to his feet. By that time, Pete and Abby were standing on the lift heading up to the hanger deck. Once they were out of the hangers. They ran to a small supply building, where they shut off speed dial. Pete told Abby that he had sent a message that we would be transporting the Anshar and Kinshar back to Gmack, and I had asked for the location to send them to. A captain of their Space Travel Command, replied back to me, and gave the coordinates on Gmack. Abby told Pete, "that was good thinking, and I'm proud of you for doing this with me". Pete smiled, and then they heard an alarm going off around the entire base, loud sirens that indicated a security breach within the complex. Guards began running around and you could here a squad of men coming up next to the building. The two of them commanded "go home" to the Magic phone, and with a whoosh, they were gone. Just then, the door flew open and a team of security police, wielding machine guns, entered the building looking for the people who were involved at taking the bodies of the two aliens.

Both Abby and Pete returned home safely, and later on the news that night, there were reports that unknown subject(s) breached the security at Area 51, and the Federal government was investigating. The reporter asked the commander of the base, if anything was taken during this breach, and his reply was, "that information is Top Secret, and I'm not at liberty to say". "All I can say is that we are looking into any clues that we can find and that we are looking through hours of security video, to help us find the perpetrator or perpetrators. Abby received a text from Pete, with a smiley face on it, and he said, don't worry, and make sure you don't tell anyone. Abby replied Ok. She then got a call from Pete. Abby said "hello" and Pete told Abby that he heard from the captain of the Space Travel Command on Gmack, and that they received the bodies of their fallen astronauts. Abby became excited and told Pete "that was great"! He then told her that the world leader would like us to visit their planet as soon as we can. They would like to personally thank us for returning Anshar and Kinshar back to their people and to their families, and that they are very grateful. He told her that an Earth representative of Gmack would be meeting with us as soon as possible. Abigail asked, "What is an Earth representative"? Pete told her that there are people, from Gmack, integrated throughout society that report to their leaders on the activities here on earth. "Wow, I had no idea that this was going on", exclaimed Abby. Then, she asked, "so does this mean we are going to Gmack"? Pete chuckled and said, "yes, this will be our first trip to Gmack, and you will be treated like royalty for what you have done for them"! Abigail said that she didn't want all that and didn't want any attention for helping them out. She stated that she just wanted to do what was right. Pete said that he had to go now, and that he would stay in touch with her. He told her to enjoy the rest of her summer vacation, and if she wanted to stop by, that she could anytime.

Chapter Fifteen

Summer Vacation

A few weeks had past since she last talked with Pete, and Abby was getting antsy; she needed another adventure to go on. It was summer and she also wanted to go on a vacation with the family. Abigail got together with Chad and Shelby to discuss another fun family vacation. Chad said that he wanted to still go to Myrtle Beach. He also said that he wouldn't mind going to Disney World too. Abby and Shelby said that we should try to do both. The kids decided on going to Disney World first and then travel up to Myrtle Beach for a few days, but they would have to discuss this with mom and dad first. When they got home after work, the kids talked to them about the possibility of going to Disney and then to Myrtle Beach. Phillip and Susan thought that the vacation plans were great, but it would take them a few weeks to get the time off from work. The kids burst out into cheer and began planning for their trip. The two weeks went by fast and before they knew it, it was time to head on down to Florida.

Abigail wanted to invite Pete and Tillie, but wasn't able to get a hold of them on the phone, or by text, for the past two weeks. She was beginning to worry and she knew that it wasn't like Pete, not to call her back. While her dad was loading the minivan, she decided to teleport over to

Pete and Tillie's house to see if they were home. When she arrived, she noticed that the house didn't look right. The drapes and blinds were no longer in the windows. When she looked in through the front window, she noticed that all of the furniture was gone. She tried to open the front door, but it was locked. Abby then tried the back door and it was locked too. So, she teleported into the house and began looking around. So many thoughts began to whirl through her mind. She thought that maybe Pete or Tillie weren't doing well and one of them was in the hospital, or maybe a secret government agency may have taken them away and that they would be coming after her next, or that they went into hiding after they infiltrated Area 51. While thinking about all the different possibilities, Abby heard some movement. She slowly walked from the kitchen into the edge of the living room and she heard the noise again. She looked over at the front door and saw that the doorknob was moving. Someone was attempting to get into the house. Abigail became frightened and froze in her spot as the door opened. A man and a woman entered into the house and they looked up to see this young lady standing in their living room. The two of them were in their mid twenties, but looked familiar to Abigail. When the two of them realized it was Abby, they smiled at her and she smiled back. Abigail's phone rang and she looked down to see who it was. She answered it and her dad asked her to get home, because they were all packed up and ready to go. Abby said that she would be right there and hung up the phone. She apologized to the couple and told them that she would be back soon, and walked out of the house.

Abigail returned home and everyone was ready to leave for the trip. Phillip had the family get into the minivan and then Abigail asked everyone to hold on to each other, while Phillip and Susan held onto the door handles.

Abby opened up her phone to the Planet earth app, and already had the coordinates of the parking lot at Disney set. She asked if everyone was ready, and they all replied "yes"! And with a Whoosh, they were gone!

Chapter Sixteen

MDF, Magic Data Files

Magic Data Files - Instructions on the capabilities and how to use your Magic Phone. Updates will be performed on an occasional basis. Along with software and application updates, the MDF files will be updated as well.

This phone's exterior is made of a titanium based alloy for high strength and light weight. There is no glass on the front or back to break. So where is the screen? The screen is made of a carbon nano-material, transparent film layer, that lights up when the phone is turned on, thus allowing the applications to be seen. When the phone is turned off, the phone appears screen-less, revealing the alloy case. The ergonomic design of the phone is unique and allows the phone to fit into the users hand with more surface to surface contact, decreasing the chance of dropping the phone and relieving pressure points on the hand. Within the finger grooves are four laser scanners that detect finger prints and the users DNA for security measures. Above the index finger position is a laser that can be used for various reasons, see below for a full description of the lasers capabilities. At the thumb position, you will find the only mechanical button on the phone. This can be used to activate the phone to turn it on or to fire the laser.

1.0 - Planet Earth:

This application allows the user to view the world from your home or to see towns, cities, countries, and places you would love to visit, but never could before. Within the app are several buttons and fields that you can use to interact with the app. There is a search field, Where Am I button, Go To button, and a Home button.

The search field allows you to Type in an address, a business, a town or a city and the application will search for your request.

The "Where Am I?" button will show where you are located on the map.

1.1 - The "Go To" button will take you to this location, tele-transporting you there in the blink of an eye. Don't worry, when this button is activated, it will take you to a safe location in the area that you chose. If you plan on taking someone on your trip with you "Be Careful" you have to hold onto that person tightly or hold their hand tightly. If you leave with someone, be sure to bring that person back home with you! It is advised, for safety reasons, to travel alone!

1.2 - The "Go Home" button is exactly what you think it means. When you press this button the phone will return you safely to your home, or you can tell the phone "Go Home".

2.0 - Calendar Application:
The calendar is an app that allows the user to set appointments, plan vacation dates, and schedule their time for current and future events. The calendar can also be used as a way to travel back and forward through time. First, lets become familiar with the tabs in the calendar. When you first open up calendar you will see the current month. At the top of the screen, you will notice the three tabs. Day, Month, and Year. The three tabs allow you to view the calendar in a day, month, and year format. Once you have found the date to make an appointment, just tap the day. Once you have selected a date that particular day will open up to a full screen and one tab will open at the top "Add". The add tab will allow you to schedule an appointment for the day you have selected.
2.1 - The bottom third of the screen is titled "Time Travel" and within this area of the screen you will see one active tab "Set Date" and two inactive tabs titled "Go" and

"Return". Tap the Set date tab and a screen will come up with several fields, (All fields must be completed to continue through all the steps). The first field is date. Tap this field and a date wheel will appear. Scroll into future years or past years and tap to select the year. The next field will allow you to enter the month and the third field will allow you to select the day. Once the date is set, you must enter the time of day, scroll to the time and select am or pm. The next field is a safety feature, which will return you back to your current date and time at home. The default setting is set to 48 hours, but you can change the time from one hour up to 96 hours. This field cannot be left blank and if left blank the Go tab will not become active. This is set for your safety, because there may be a time when you can't get to your phone and hit return home manually. While you are traveling and you need to get home right at that moment, bring up the calendar and tap "Return". This will bring you back to your current time and location.

2.2 - No time will have passed in the present, while you are traveling. The next field is location. When you tap this field, the calendar will disappear and Planet Earth will than appear. This will allow you to find the area you would like to travel to. Enter the place in the search field and the app will show you your selected location. Then, you can tap on an exact area to be located. Once you have tapped over the place of destination a blue cross will appear. Click on the "Done" tab and you will be returned back to the calendar screen. You will now see that the "Go" tab is lit up, which means that it is active. When you click on this tab, HOLD ON TIGHT, because you will travel through time at the speed of light.

2.3 - While on your travels, if you tap the "Return Home" tab, you will come back to the exact location and time that you left from. In addition, if you are sent back from the default time limit, initiating your return, you will come back to the exact location and time that you left from. If you have any questions, please contact Pete. My information can be found in the directory, and I don't mind showing you how to do this operation safely.

2.4 - Time Clock: Is a feature that will allow the user to change their age, but you can only change your age backwards; so, if you would like to go back to a younger you, you can adjust this dial clock found in the calendar application. If you don't see it in the calendar app. that means you are not fifty years old yet, and that will be the age where your phone is updated with this accessory. Once you have it installed on the Magic Phone, you can spin the clock in one-minute increments, and for every minute, you will be decreasing your age by one year. There are sixty minutes on the clock; therefore, you can decrease your age by sixty years at max. If you are fifty years old when you first use this add on, you will note that there are only thirty minutes highlighted and only highlighted minutes will be available for you to use. Simply put, you cannot decrease your age to less than 20 years of age. Sorry, but safety is very important when it comes to time travel. In addition, if you decrease your age but don't change the date, you will become younger. This can be reversed, but time and space continue on at the normal rate, while you are younger. Therefore, if you stay young for one year and return the dial back to zero, you will come back at one year older. Things that you should be aware of: if you decide to become younger, your family and friends will not recognize you. So, you will either have to alienate yourself from your family or you will have some serious explaining to do! Also, you could continue this process and live for quite a long time. How long? Nobody knows!

2.5 - Helpful hints:

- When you travel, it would be best to dress the part. There is an app that allows you to get the clothing of your choice based on the area and time period that you will be going to. Find Clothing under the Magic App.

- Currency is another app that will be useful while traveling through time. This app will get you some money based on the location and time period and will dispense the appropriate amount for you to use, based on the time period. See 7.0 - 7.1 in this appendix.

- Hold on to your phone and don't let anyone hold it or even see it!!!

- Keep your earpiece in and you can communicate with the phone while it is secure in your pocket. Your clothing should always have a pocket that can be buttoned down or zipped.

2.6 - The phone can be submerged to a depth of 500 meters or dropped from a height of approximately 50 feet with no harm to the external or internal components.

3.0 - Gateway browser and the "Time Search" Engine:
The Time Search engine is a tool that you use within the web browser application "Gateway", which can allow you to search an infinite amount of information from the past,

present, and future. However, the future is continuous and not totally explored by the creator of this application; therefore, it is currently limited to approximately 175 years into the future. Sorry for the inconvenience. Future updates will be automatically uploaded and an email of the update will be sent to your inbox.

If you know how to use a search engine, this will be very easy to master! Just type in a topic into the search field within the Gateway app, and tap enter; your information will come up within seconds. For example, type into the search field "who is the president of the United States in the year 2063"? Within a few seconds the answer and its sources will begin to fill the page.

4.0 - Weather Application:

The weather App is designed with ease in mind. You can check the weather worldwide at anytime. The weather is updated every 15 minutes so that the most current information is provided. This App allows the user to check local, national, and world weather conditions. It will also allow the user to access current weather, future weather, and manipulate the weather. Once in the Application, start by selecting your current location, or the location that you're inquiring about. Seven locations can be saved. For the weather, you can access different panes: hourly weather for the upcoming 24 hours, monthly weather conditions, and yearly weather in a calendar format. Tap on the applicable weather pane and then select the date you are inquiring about. Don't forget to insert the correct location at the top of the window.

4.1 - At the bottom of the display, you will see a tab that states, "Change weather". When you tap on this pane, you will have access to several weather patterns for the currently selected location.

a. Sunny - High Pressure

b. Cloudy - Decreasing pressure

c. Rain - Low Pressure

4.2 - Below the weather patterns is a temperature slide. This allows you to select the temperature you are looking for. To the left of the slide you will see -5 degrees in Celsius and incremental steps of five degrees increasing up to 40 degrees Celsius at the far right of the scale. If you prefer Fahrenheit, go to settings - weather- temperature scale and tap Fahrenheit.

4.3 - Once these parameters are set, tap the confirm tab at the bottom right of the screen. The weather will take one to two hours to change to the selected weather pattern. Also, the weather pattern will continue for approximately ten hours.

4.4 - As a side note, you cannot change night hours into sunny hours. This is limited to the daytime only for your selected area.

4.5 - When you select a rainy pattern, you will see a slide rule at the bottom of the screen, just below the temperature slide rule. The amount of rain can be selected from a minimum of 2/10" per hour to 1" per hour. The rain will continue for approximately four hours. If you select a temperature below 0 degrees Celsius the rain will turn to snow.

5.0 - Clothing Application:
The clothing App can be used as a stand alone or within the Calendar App. The clothing App can put you into any clothes that are accessible within the clothing app or in the Gateway app by searching clothing. To accept money/currency, you must be wearing clothing created from this application. The currency that is provided will appear in a closed "Magic" pocket in your clothing. There is no other way to delver your currency at this time.
5.1 - When you select this application, you have access to thousands of outfits and accessories that can be worn simply by selecting the clothing and clicking on the change tab. You can select clothing by type, styles, and by time periods. The clothing is tied into the calendar app, which will allow you to select your clothing prior to departing on your trip in time. Have fun with this app, dress up, and Halloween will never be the same.

6.0 - Magic Wand:

The magic wand app uses the energy from the universe and channels it to manipulate your surroundings. It has energy to over come gravity, elevating objects or yourself into the air; thus, allowing you to fly. The laser, found on the top of leading edge of the phone, above the ergonomic finger holds, can act as a stunning light or intensified to cut through all types of objects including thick metals. You can use the wand to push or pull an object. It has a protective shield that you can use either on the ground or in the air. The magic wand can also temporarily stun, freeze, or even turn a person into stone. The wand will also erase the memory from a person so that they cannot remember what happened to them, found as a camera function.

6.1 - You can open the magic wand by tapping on the applications tab on the main screen or by saying, "open Magic Wand" into the phone or into your ear mic, when the phone is on. With the recent upgrade (4/12/13), the voice activation is continuous and the phone does not have to be on. Once the app is opened, you activate powers by voice commands and hand gestures. Once the magic wand app is activated, the phone stays on until the app is closed. During these operations, you may feel a temperature difference with the phone because it can get much warmer with extended time and use, because so much power is required for this application. The app has the following tabs: Fly, Freeze, Laser, Lift-Lower, Push/Pull, Shield.

6.2 - Voice Commands include: Fly, lift, down, Push, pull, stun, freeze, turn to stone, laser intensity low, laser intensity medium, laser intensity high, and shield me.

6.3 - Hand gestures: During flight mode, lifting your hands upward will increase the speed of lift and flight, lowering your hands will slow your speed and decrease lift allowing you to land, lifting one hand higher than the other will allow you to turn, i.e. raise your left hand higher will cause you to turn to the right. Moving your trunk forward, flexing forward at the abdominals, will change your flight path forward from an upright position, or downward from a horizontal position; extending at the trunk will change your flight path backward/upward, depending on your orientation. It's recommended that you keep the phone in a secure pocket during flight, see helpful hints. When you have commanded lift, push, or pull, point the back of the phone towards the object you wish to move. You will see objects in the screen where the phone will automatically lock onto the predominant feature on the screen, or you can touch the screen to manually lock onto the item you want to move. Next, your hand movement will move your object in the same direction and at the same rate of speed that your arms move. i.e. Voice command is "lift" hand and arm gestures are upward. If you want to lower an object, the voice command "down" is used along with a hand gesture moving downward, and push or pull to move the object forward or backward. If you push or pull very fast it will throw the object. When your voice command is stun, freeze, turn to stone, you have to point to the person or object you are effecting. With the voice command laser and its intensity, you have to point the back camera lens at the object that you would like to fire at. The laser will fire at a two-second burst, unless you hold down the fire button.

6.4 - Shield: Is the only voice command that doesn't require a hand gesture to control its operation, and when you fly, travel into space, tele-transport, time shift, and time travel, the shield is automatically activated. To shield yourself, all you have to do is shout, "shield me" and a powerful force field will surround your body. This shield can deflect a person's fist, bullets, high intensity laser beams, extreme heat created from extreme speed, a car, a train, and even a meteorite flying through the atmosphere and landing on you. So basically, it can protect you from just about anything!

6.5 - Flight school: Tap on the hyperlink *flight school* and the flight tutorial will begin teaching you how to fly, step by step. Be sure to find a wide-open area for your first few flights, safety first.

6.6 - Laser: within the Magic App, is the Laser tab. When this is selected, you will have three options of intensity. Select the intensity for the desired effect or for defense. Using this application for offensive purposes requires a lot of careful consideration. Nevertheless, the three levels include low, medium, and high. Low intensity is used for stunning a person, causing them to drop to the ground for 20-30 seconds. It can also be used to cut through light thin objects. Medium intensity will cause a mild burning effect and incapacitate the person for about 5 minutes depending on the persons morphology. For example, a large man weighing in at 300 lbs, would experience incapacitation for about 4 minutes. Where a person who is approximately 200 lbs, would be incapacitated for the 5 minutes. Also, a person who is only a hundred pounds would be incapacitated for about 6 minutes. It can also be used to cut through heavier materials such as wood, plastics, and cloth materials. High intensity, if used on an animal or human will cause death. In addition, it will cut through all metal objects, armor, thick steel plating, titanium, kevlar, and carbon fiber. To properly aim the laser, look along the top edge of the phone, keeping the leading and trailing edges lined up with each other. Press the thumb button and the laser will fire at the selected intensity for as long as you hold the thumb button down. If you press and release the thumb button, the laser will fire at a 2-3 second burst, depending on the selected intensity. This will assist in giving the desired effect based on your selected intensity.

6.7 - Helpful hints: You can combine commands or add commands while in another command. Multitasking can occur with all commands. For instance, if you activated the shield, you can incorporate your laser, or you could command that an oncoming car to be pushed away from you. While in flight and above an object that is falling to the ground, you can command pull and slow the object for a soft landing on the ground. The multitasking is endless and will improve with time and practice. It is recommended that you keep your Magic phone in a pocket from an outfit designed by the clothing app. This will keep your phone secure in a pocket designed specifically for the phone, and will also allow for excellent reception to track body movements. Placing the phone in a pocket made from denim, for instance, will degrade the signal and may interrupt movement patterns causing the commands to respond erratically.

7.0 - Currency Application:

This app allows you to use money in current times, in the past, and in the future. The money will appear, in small quantities, within the pocket of any clothing created by the Magic Phone. Currency will not appear in store bought clothing. What is the definition of small quantities of currency? In the year of 2013, when you request money you will receive $100.

7.1 - If you travel back in time to the year 1913, you will receive $4.25. Travel back to 1963 and you will receive $13.14. If more money is needed, you will have to text Pete the amount needed and the reasons for the increase in money. If approved, the money will appear in your magic pocket.

8.0 - Translator Application:

The translator allows the user to talk into the built in microphone or the earpiece, when paired to the phone, and have their sentences translated. Open up the application and select language that you are speaking. Then, select the language to be translated. Once these two selections are made the green "Translate" tab becomes activated. You can now speak into the microphone and the translation will commence from your phone's speaker. If the person you are speaking with begins talking, the translator will pick up his or her sentences and translate them for you. The sentence will be displayed in writing and heard via the speaker.

8.1 - Helpful hints: When your or the person you are speaking with are talking, make sure they are within two feet to insure language accuracy. If you are unsure of the person's language, tap the analyze tab at the bottom right of the Translator screen. Have the person speak into the phone's microphone and their voice will be analyzed. Once analyzed, the language will be displayed and activate the translate tab automatically. If you find yourself in a situation where a language is displayed in writing, tap on the photo analyze tab. Point the camera towards the displayed language and the Magic phone will determine the language and interpret the writings for you.
8.2 - The Translator is good for all languages on earth, including the planet Gmack. There is also a very large library of words for more accurate translations.

9.0 - Food & Water: Food and water can be delivered to you at a moments notice. Open up the application from your home screen and select your choices of foods and drinks. You have many choices from healthy snacks to breakfast, lunch, and dinner combos. There is one requirement for this application to work for you though. This operation requires you to have the Magic Pack, which is similar to the Magic Pocket where you receive your money. The magic pack is big enough to receive most meals. If your meal is too big for the pack, the meal will be broken down in size. Once you pull the portion of the meal delivered, close the pack and zip it shut. The remainder of the meal will be delivered very shortly. Keep in mind, that when you are traveling, it is important to drink plenty of water. For most people, sixty-four ounces of water a day is recommended. Give this feature a try; it's a lot of fun!!

10.0 - Medic App:

The magic phone has a medic app. that can scan all body functions, make an assessment from the data, diagnose your condition, and automatically send you the best possible medication to treat your symptoms. The Magic pack is required for this application as well, because medication, disinfectant, bandages, gauze, tape, splints, etc… will be delivered to the magic pack.

10.1 - If you are injured in your travels, run the scan in the Medic App. Once your are diagnosed, if it is recommended, the phone will suggest a treatment option. If a laser treatment is recommended, the phone will ask you to point the laser at the wound site. A small red light will emit from the laser so that it is pointed at the target area. Once you are lined up, tap the clean tab and the laser will do the rest. When the laser automatically stops, wrap the wound with the bandages in your

Magic pack as soon as possible, one minute or less is recommended.

11.0 - Cloaking:

The Cloaking device, when activated, will form a thin electromagnetic field around you, and within seconds it will reach the appropriate frequency to render you invisible. There are three tabs that may be selected once the app is running, Cloak, Stop, and Identity. To start the cloaking process, open the app. Tap on the cloak tab and within seconds you will be invisible. To deactivate the Cloaker, just tap on the stop button from within the app. When you are cloaked, be sure to turn off the screen to avoid tapping the Stop tab. That would not be good in any situation.

11.1 - Identity - If you decide that an identity change is needed, you can tap the identity tab. Your identity selection will come up by categories. The first category is gender {male or female}. Once you've made your selection, select the desired nationality by scrolling through the list. Once you've selected nationality, a folder with thousands of photos will populate the screen. Select the photo that you would like to look like and the cloaking device will take care of the rest. You will be cloaked with an image displayed via the cloak, similar to a hologram, but much more lifelike.

12.0 - Camera:

The camera can be used to take fun photos and video for all occasions. You can select vertical or horizontal modes depending on the orientation of the camera. The camera has flash options: on, off, automatic, step up, or step down. If step up or down are selected for the flash, you can step up the intensity by three increments, each increment will make the flash stronger for darker situations, or step the flash down in three increments to decrease the amount of flash. This could be used to allow for a fill flash effect, for close subjects, when there is sufficient ambient light. At the top left of the screen, is a button that allows for shutter priority. Shutter priority allows the photographer increased control over the amount of light that is exposed on the sensor, which can increase light exposure in low light situations or increase speed for subjects that are moving fast, like a football player running down the field. Decreasing shutter speed will require increased control over the camera to prevent blurring.

12.1 - IR "Infrared" allows the user to see in low light and dark conditions. When you open the camera app, scroll the wheel to IR. The phone now becomes your night vision phone. You can use this feature to navigate in dark places and you can take pictures in total darkness. Do not use the IR feature in daylight, because it can destroy the sensor.

12.1.1 - Night vision (IR) glasses. To activate the SFD "Spectacle Forward Display" go into settings. Tap the SFD tab and move the slider to the on position. The glasses will pair with the Magic Phone. These spectacles allow the user to see in the darkest of situations. They also allow the user to see the phones display through the lenses of the glasses. You can operate the phone while looking at the glasses both tacitly or in conjunction with the voice commands. The spectacles include a microphone built into the right ear piece and speakers are built into both ear pieces.

12.2 - Memory eraser:

There may come a time when someone sees you using the Magic phone. When this occurs, you may need to erase their memory of this event, because you don't want anyone to know about the technology that you have. Many people are greedy and will want to steal the phone and technology from you, especially the government. They are always looking for new technology and ways to spy on us. It's easy to access the memory eraser, just open up the camera app on your phone. Just above the photo button, you will see a scrolling wheel. The wheel has four options on it, photo, video, IR, and erase. When you select Erase, it prepares the camera to emit a flash that looks similar to the flash from a camera. However, this flash of light will cause the mind to go blank and erase the last fifteen minutes of their memory. The person will be in a daze for about one minute and will return to their normal selves at that point.

13.0 - Speed Dial - this application will allow you to manipulate the time by allowing the user to increase their speed. When you open this application, you will see a basic screen with a horizontal bar (slide rule) in the center of the screen. There are ten increments on the slide with slower to the left of the slide and faster further to the right of the slide rule. The range of speed at the low end is slightly faster than where you normally would move. You will perceive movement around you as slightly slower. Be sure to try and talk a little slower and move slower to be perceived as having normal speed to those around you, when needed. If you move the slide rule all the way to the right, the change in speed will max out at just over half the speed of light. When you reach this high rate of speed, your watch will show a count of 60 seconds to the clock in the world around you at 1 second. That means you would have to stand still for 30 seconds before someone could see you for a split second. Fast!!! Once you have the speed selected, the start tab will become active; tap that tab when you are ready to start. Note: Once you move the slide rule more than 3 clicks, the shield is active during the duration of your time shift.

14.0 - Security:

This device comes with the best security system available to man. Once the phone has a profile of your biometrics, if any other person carries it for more than fifteen minutes, it will set off a silent alarm. The manufacturer (Pete or Tilly) will answer the alarm and take your phone from the perpetrator and return it to you or your safe spot.

15.0 - Just Speak: Release date 4/12/2014.

Just speak is an update that allows the user not only to speak and communicate with the Magic Phone, but to also listen to the phone continuously. This feature can be turned off, but it is not advised to. Just speak allows the user to receive updates on happenings, dangers, severe weather changes, or imminent danger in your area. Just speak allows the user to speak into the ear piece microphone, that is built into the supplied ear ring, which will allow you to communicate continuously and quickly with the Magic Phone. You can verbalize all of your commands now without opening an application, and the phone will detect, analyze, and learn your communicating behaviors to adjust and improve efficiency the more you use it.

15.1 - Helpful Hints: Begin communicating to the phone and ask it questions. i.e. what will the weather be like tomorrow, who will be the seventy-first president, camera, shield, cloak, night vision, push away, lift, fly. etc... The commands are endless.

16.0 - Games - This is a 4D world, that allows the user to experience training to improve skills with all tasks that this phone offers, including hundreds of scenarios that could be encountered as the user of the Magic Phone. In addition to training, the user could experience ferry tales, racing, traveling, flying aircraft, space flight, and sports.

The End

About The Author

Gary Welch has lived on Long Island since 1998 with his family. This is the first novel that he's written and it's based on a dream that his daughter had in 2012. "During the year that it took me to write this novel, I felt like I was on the greatest adventure I could ever imagine. "At times, I felt like I really owned this phone and had hit the lottery, because of all its magical powers that it offered Abigail and our family.

Gary has a doctorate degree in physical therapy and owns a clinic in Patchogue NY with his wife. He also manages a physical therapy department that he started at a National Laboratory back in 1998.

Gary is an adjunct professor at Stony Brook University and Touro College, here on Long Island, where he wrote the course work "Manual and Manipulative Therapy of the Spine and Pelvis.

Dr. Welch plans to continue writing the sequel to the Magic Phone. So, stay tuned for more adventures as Abigail gets older and her adventures become more intense. You can follow The Magic phone on the website http//:www.abbysmagicphone.com and on Facebook www.facebook.com/themagicphone

About the Illustrator

Wesley Lowe has been a freelance artist for many years and has created art for companies such as National Geographic, Harlequin Books, Bantam Books, and many other publishers and advertising agencies. His greatest passion is for painting aviation, marine, and historical subjects, which he devotes most of his free time to. His medium of choice is oil paint on canvas.

CPSIA information can be obtained at www.ICGtesting.com
Printed in the USA
BVOW06s2105280915

419994BV00002B/6/P